THE SILENCE

Barry Barnett Keith

authorHouse®

AuthorHouse™
1663 Liberty Drive, Suite 200
Bloomington, IN 47403
www.authorhouse.com
Phone: 1-800-839-8640

First published by AuthorHouse 4/14/2009

ISBN: 978-1-4389-5951-1 (sc)

*Printed in the United States of America
Bloomington, Indiana*

This book is printed on acid-free paper.

For Cam and Baby

Miss Ella

Thank You
For Your Faith

Psalm 141: 4-6 **The Bible**

ONE

August, 2050

"ASHES TO ASHES, dust to dust," Pastor Jenkins spat out against a swirling, hot wind. He held his hands to his chest, along with a small, worn copy of The Bible with his long, processed hair blowing back and forth. The oblong, plain wooden coffin containing Ronnie Carson sat on straps, ready to be lowered into a hole dug into the ground. Off to one side, were two grave diggers leaning on their shovels, impatient, standing still out of respect, but ready to move on to the next plot and there were many to be tended to. "We pray that the life of this young man has been pleasing in your sight, Lord. And now servant, rest."

The Pastor then turned to Deacon Carson. "Frank, would you like to say a word?"

Carson cleared his throat, emerging partially out of the cocoon of sadness gripping him.

"Ronnie…I'll always love you little buddy. I'll always remember the things we used to do. I'll remember all the times you laughed, and all the times you cried and all those times you snuggled up against me at night for protection. God will protect you now. I can still see and remember those times we went to the movies together, and all the times we shot basketball together. Son, you were one heck of a player, and even more of a person. It's funny you know, I'm just now realizing that sports was something we just happened to do, while we talked about right and wrong and our love for life." Carson paused for a moment and closed his eyes, still expecting to wake up from the whole ordeal. He opened his eyes again to the ashen color of disappointment smothering the barren plains, and the box still sat before him along with the quiet, sobering sound of the whistling wind, telling him how absolutely nothing had changed.

"Even more than that son, you were my life. You and your mama will always be my best friends, and I know you two will always walk with the Lord, like you did here on earth. I'll see you both soon. Remember, I love you."

"This concludes the services for this young man today. You all may leave now," the undertaker said, placing his hand upon Carson's shoulder.

"If you need me for anything, you know where I am," Pastor Jenkins whispered to Carson. Pastor Jenkins' father was a preacher, and his father before him. He was a complete throwback to the early days of "old time religion," with his processed hair and gigantic pores on a big, sleepy face revealing evidence of an ongoing battle with one or several vices over the course of many years. Pastor Jenkins usually wore outfits made up of pieces of other suits- arbitrary choices of a plaid jacket here, striped pants there, patterned shirts and even paisley ties. Always fighting against what he considered to be the "great force of evil" dominating the people of the reservation, he carried that faded copy of the Holy Bible with him at all times. *Great force of evil? Wow, you have no idea. Then again old man, you just might.* Whenever he shook his head out of disappointment in front of his screaming, entertainment starved congregation of The Baptist Church of The Reservation, he did it to express his true dissatisfaction with the spiritual direction of his people. For anyone truly paying attention, under his crusty surface Pastor Jenkins was more than just an old, fading preacher with no sense of style. He cared for everyone with all his heart and he truly believed in God, even if no one else around him would. Carson considered him a friend and would not have wanted anyone else on the hill with him that day; a man whom he knew was liberated from the opinions and thoughts of others.

The few others who stood on the hill- Miss Latise from down at the corner store who continued to serve with a smile, Pastor Jenkins who helped Carson to mentor kids in the community, Derrick Valentine down the road- a mechanic who was known to work on a car or two for free just to help someone out and Maria and Anna, two of the sweetest young people from the church Ronnie had befriended- were all Carson had left. Besides Pastor Jenkins, he came to see the young ones as his own children.

All of them stood beside me, silently watching the tears on my face and my revelation of how the great flood that nearly devastated our reservation three months before continued to expose worms and the steaming stench of inequities in life. My name is Carson, Frank Carson. I serve as a Deacon at The Baptist Church of The Reservation. I realize no man would ever want to bury his own son, least of all, me. Ronnie was one of the many who fell to the disease the deluge left behind. We stood under some of the wilting trees on the gated, infertile plains we call home. The trees swayed back and forth through the light wind while cracked, unknowing, singular weeds bend against the odor of traffic trudging by toward the outside world. I stood there on the hill nearly alone as a result of consequence; by caring for an uncaring world and expecting it would care for me in return. When a member of the congregation needed me, I was always there. In the beginning, I blindly ran for others thinking I would gain favor with The Lord at the end of my life, my time here on earth. Once Ronnie got sick and passed away, I became angry with The Lord, and I had to ask myself why I did I ever want to serve others in the first place- if it was not to gain some sort of advantage over other men?

Everyone walked away, and only Carson remained, standing over the box containing much of his life, along with the ditch that awaited it. Feeling the scolding temperature of the summer wind against his face, he was uncertain about a great many things.

Carson stood nearly alone because most of the funerals he had ever been to, even before the flood, he never really knew any of the families until it was too late, until trouble was upon their door. Once families were given to him in the church to care for, he introduced himself, and pleaded with them to call upon him should they ever need anything. They all just smiled and their smiles all said the same thing; "I am not in pain right now, and if there is no pain, there is really no need to call on you, God or anyone else." He wrote cards and letters to many sharing the good news of The Coming of The Lord, but he never received one response.

"He will send someone to me in time, in his time," Carson reasoned over the years.

By the sound of a line of revving engines a short distance away, Carson heard how the cars were more concerned over a desperate tear toward their destinations, meaningless in the end. *His* son was dead, and all they could think of was where they were *going*. The fact of the matter was, Ronnie was just one of many to die, but Carson could not see that. *How did you die son- you were only twelve years old? How does God permit these kinds of things to happen?* Ronnie was someone without fear- the little guy loved everybody. Carson would always remember his laugh which soothed and tormented him, tempting him to call God out. Ronnie was not one who was seduced by the new drug, like so many other decadent ones who stood in the shadows of night throughout the reservation, working for The Specter of Evil. Many of the young on the plains walked aimlessly through flying trash strewn about the plains daily to their drug induced deaths wanting to convince anyone at all to come with them because they feared being alone; they just wished for a hand to hold. It was too late for many once they discovered The Specter was actually lying to them about forging toward a better way of life by ignoring their own lives on earth.

Through Carson's own experience years before with waiting for The Specter to claim his life from the mundane color of the weight of love's disappointments and life's responsibilities, he still felt how the horrible, menacing being waited in darkness for his soul that was unwilling and unable to find light. Day and night, Carson took in the new drug, while his very life on earth evaporated within hallucinogenic clouds of smoke the evil being presented to him as doorways to freedom. *I was so close to dying. So close to turning my back on the creator, forever.* Since Carson overcame the beast, it became his mortal enemy, pursuing him through the years, taking the life of his wife, then his son. The Specter was alive and Carson knew that the intent of the being was to strip the plains, the people, the spirit and the love from around him until he stood alone. Carson decided to find faith in The Lord, or fall; he knew he could not fight the being alone. The Specter lived within a vulgar mentality away from human dreams and courage and he salivated for the ever growing numbers who gave up on God and life itself. To the unknowing, The Specter appeared seductive as sugar and spice, sweet chocolate or soft marshmallows or even the flavor of hot, fresh baked apple pie. Ronnie had the courage to believe in God, the Alpha and the Omega- the one who was responsible for everything. Why then, was he made to suffer, in front of the many here who stand in defiance of any consequences of the lives they lead?

The "NO TRESSPASSING" sign dangled off to the side of the main gate of the reservation each day which was part of the giant, rusted fence which could not hold back the rain. After the waters came, there were many gaping holes in the fence where any intruder might come and go as he wished. All the people on the reservation believed the same thing; "Why would anyone want to come here, besides gambling?" To look around, there were holes in roofs exposing worn ebony paper and broken supports, along with paint chipping away from wood surfaces that had long ago surrendered to the environment as well as the weight of their inhabitants. Makeshift clotheslines with faded colors of khaki, sienna, rose and dingy fabrics that used to be colored titanium waved through the hot, humid wind. A beaten, muddy front of a "loans until payday" business that also served a gathering place for corner drinkers, drug sellers and soapbox preachers had finally closed its doors. The motley crew who used to stand in front of it did not like change, but like roaches, their mentality adjusted and they moved on to survive elsewhere, away from the reservation on the roads or behind other abandoned huts to alleyways here and there. The sun drenched houses, dilapidated from the flood, all looked up to scorching skies over an infertile land; a corner torn from a world the patchwork community within called home. The shanties and their dwellers rendered themselves insignificant in accordance with the expectations of the outside world, and the flood had only further revealed those things had been true for decades. There were still people missing on the reservation, yet the highest priority from the government was to get the casino up and running because it was an unsaid fact among the people that to endure day by day without a public place to gamble would be too much to bear. Bruised and neglected, the houses leaned against one another beside broken, pothole filled dirt roads wondering when they would ever find relief in the form of a merciful God and a changed mentality among their destructive inhabitants. Carson had no answer for them.

Carson thought he was perhaps a fool to believe in something greater than everyone who ever walked the earth combined as he stood in silence atop the largest hill, feeling the collective soul of everyone below slowly dying. He looked out upon many paths of dirt and mud below covered with the footprints of the lost, the forlorn and the forgotten. Carson believed *they* were God's people, though the church had a hard time convincing them of that. Many chose to remain ignorant and ready to be pushed around with a governmental swipe of a pen or pencil. The people on the plains had cheated, misinformed and abused themselves and their children-swayed by the arousing colors and special effects of the outside world to feel less than. As a result, children wandered all over the reservation; pulled into the drug trade, panhandling around the casino or playing with balls given to them by their parents who were determined to push them toward being professional ball players, hoping that feat would not take much effort as a byproduct of being black.

TWO

"COME ON, HILL! You can do better than that!" Coach Turk yelled. ""Jesus Christ, man, what I gotta do ta' make you hit somebody!"

"I'm trying coach!" Vince pleaded. "Let me back in, I'll do better!"

"Go ahead!" Coach yelled again. "Try not ta' get pinned against the bar this time!"

Vince pushed the player waiting in front of him out of the way, and got back into the cage. The cage was an apparatus Coach Turk used to see how quickly individual players responded to the football once it was snapped up from the ground. The device was simply a bunch of steel bars welded together into a long rectangle. The rectangle was divided into six sections. In practice, the idea of the cage was that six players lined up in each individual section of the rectangle. Coach Turk stood in front of the cage with a football in his hand maniacally barking out signals. After a simulated snap of the ball, each player in the cage would fire out of his individual space. That did not seem so hard, aside from the idea of another player whose mission was to keep him inside the cage, lining up in front of him. It was just Vince's luck that he drew Mike Chambers, the strongest player on the team. He had just pinned Vince's back to the top bar of the cage as he tried to get out, even as he tried with all his might to break free.

"You gonna try me again?!" Mike yelled. "Boy I just pinned you- you want some more!?"

"Bring it, jerk! Come on, COME ON!" Vince screamed. He got down in a three-point stance in front of the cage, already fatigued. For a moment, Vince put his head down and looked down into the dead dirt of the reservation. Instead of a reprieve, the August heat and humidity rose into his facemask and inside his helmet, where it became trapped, translating into sweat, and sucking the life out of him.

"Come on Hill!" Coach Turk yelled. "Come on! Don't let him do that to you again! Don't let him talk to you like that!"

"DAMMIT!! COME ON!!" Vince yelled, slapping Mike upside his helmet and summoning all he had left. All of the other spaces within the cage were empty, because the rest of the team stood around watching, with Coach's blessing. All the seniors yelled for Mike, while all the underclassmen yelled for Vince. Mike was a bully in the locker room, and many of the underclassmen had always wanted to take him on. Vince just had the unfortunate task of doing it first. If his attempt was successful, it would open a new door for the underclassmen to challenge the seniors. It was just Mike and Vince. The promising freshman against the proven senior. "I can't let him pin me again," Vince thought. "I just can't."

"Ready set...GO!" Coach snapped the ball, and out Vince went. For a split second, Vince saw in Mike's eyes a glimmer that he took it all seriously- a glimmer of concern at how Vince just might come out of the cage. Vince came out with all of his might, and all the yelling he heard from the seniors egging Mike on around him grew silent. Once Vince made contact with him, he was just too big, too strong. Soon after Vince fired out of the cage, the back of his neck hit the top bar, and Mike held him there. Vince's legs flailed, as he tried with all his might. It wasn't even a contest, until Vince got the idea to slide underneath Mike as he looked away to gloat toward the seniors. In desperation, Vince punched him in his side and when Mike reached around to see what Vince had done, he had slid free. Just for good measure though, as Mike continued to grab his side, Vince came back around and slammed him into the bar, pinning him, to the delight of the freshmen.

"VINCE! YEAH! COME ON! GET HIM!"

For a few moments, as Vince had Mike pinned by holding one of his arms down, he wondered if

Coach was ever going to put an end to the contest. As everyone continued yelling, Vince felt his strength fading, fading with the screaming he began hearing around him that quickly became faint again. Mike slowly began turning him around, as Vince's feet began slipping on the grass, and he knew no one would except that as an excuse. Vince's back was pinned against the bar, again.

"Mike!" Coach yelled, "Let him down, he's had enough!"

"No coach! I want him to stay up there, and maybe he'll think about who he mouths off to next time!"

"Mike! Let him down!" Coach yelled again.

Mike let Vince down when Coach Turk pulled on his arm, and when Vince fell to the ground, all the seniors gathered around and laughed, while patting Mike on the back.

"Get up punk!" one of them yelled to Vince.

Vince was so mad, listening to their laughter, and seeing Mike joking about the whole thing. Vince stood up, and pulled his helmet off, his eyes ablaze with anger.

"YOU LAUGHING AT ME?!" Vince screamed, swinging his helmet and catching Mike upside his head. Mike fell to the ground.

"Hey man, you crazy or what?!" another one of the seniors yelled.

"Yeah, I'm crazy, and I'll fight all of you right now! Don't laugh at me! DON'T LAUGH AT ME!" Vince yelled.

"HILL! ARE YOU OUT OF YOUR MIND, BOY?! GET OUTTA HERE!" Coach Turk yelled, grabbing Vince by the arm and pushing him away. Vince threw his helmet across the field, because he hated them all. They made him feel like a nobody. He knew the only reason he was even playing football was because his father wanted him to. Coach Turk came up behind Vince and grabbed him by the jersey.

"You wait for me after practice, boy!" he whispered. Vince jerked away from him and headed back into the school. He heard their laughter behind him as he walked away. Their laughter burned inside him as he sat down in the hallway by Coach's office.

THREE

LOOKING DOWN ON the sparse pathways from above, Frank Carson wondered if many on the plains believed if God would ever come, because of the hopeless way they lived; rushing home after work to get drunk, ignoring their children and not even giving themselves a chance to dream or imagine their real value in their own eyes. He discerned all that from the fact it was the bells of the casino keeping time on the reservation, not the church. He was a witness on Sundays to folks coming to church for entertainment, not discipleship. At the same time, he sensed the word for a better way of life was somewhere encased in a box, in a room locked with a combination lock and only a few people who were quite reluctant to share knew where the key was. Any spirit the people held toward God on Sundays dissipated like cigarette smoke as they walked out the door to eat or to even gamble. Many who wandered upon the dirt roads never dared confront The Specter who tore at their souls, waiting for "right moments of vulnerability" to make late night sales pitches for hedonism. The community stood in financial debt to creditors who stood in moral debt to the community itself, jacking up prices on necessities, vices and suggesting advances on their already miniscule paychecks. A depression floated among the older inhabitants who transferred their past debts from drinking, smoking and gambling the nights away to the children who paid with their futures. The children watched day to day life among their parents from a short distance away and reasoned they had no reason to subscribe to any information about God, seeing how strange, drunken behavior had carried the "oldheads" such a short distance toward their hopes and dreams, sans dignity.

The reservation was a land made up of very poor gamblers whose Plan A was to win a lottery and become independent of neighbors who reminded themselves of themselves; just too nosy. Perhaps, once the winnings were secure in each individual mind on the plains, they all could move to the city and go on loud shopping sprees for unwanted things in front of others who may or may not be listening and pretend to have someplace pressing to be but is actually a reason to avoid an all important date with self. More importantly, past the chores, the stores, semi-fresh air and a make believe Times Square, turn completely bland in color and emotion like the rest in the city who got clunked on the head with the epiphany that racism was never about color, but money, with the lottery- not work- being the thing to break the aura of being an untouchable. Oh, to walk and talk like they do in the city and be as obtrusive and wasteful as the next guy, which was something they believed was a God given right. God? He would become a friend, again, once the winnings were secure, but for sure until that day Carson had a feeling the people's mentality would never realize what an actual blessing could be without the idea of money.

Every day, Frank Carson walked through the land of broken hearts, and no one knew him. He was a man in limbo, existing in a separate world between the living and the dead. He detached himself from the blue ones there who gambled, took drugs and stole so as not to continue living in a complete disappointment that would turn crimson with anger, then finally to a pale, ashen ennui. Ronnie was his only link to the living and wherever he went, his son was beside him. Outside of his little boy and the few people who stood with him on the hill, he really knew no one, until he was called upon. Even then, he was shoved aside for the Pastor, as if Pastor Jenkins, who most people on the plains really considered an old fool, could happen along and soothe lifetimes squandered away before they passed into what they hoped would be the "light." When the grave diggers lowered the box into the ground containing Ronnie, Frank Carson wondered who would finally stand to grieve over him when his own time was done? Would Jesus go down into the grave with him? *How much longer will I have to walk upon this swirling piece of rock alone, before he calls me too to rest?*

"Daddy, can I ask you somethin'? Ronnie asked, pulling on his father's sleeve.

"Of course you can," Carson replied, sensing his question might not be typical.

"What does it mean to *die* daddy?" he asked. "What happens when you die?"

"We go on to live with the Lord, son. Don't you believe that?"

He did not answer right away. "Is that what happened to mama?"

"Yeah, son, that's what happened to mama once you were born. I'm sorry you never had a chance to know your mama, she was a good woman. I know you know she loved you."

"How could she love me? She didn't even know me."

"You are a combination of me and her, born from love. She carried and protected you for nine months until you could come into this world. She gave her life so you could be born safely in this world."

"Do you miss her daddy?"

"Ronnie, there is not a day that goes by when I don't think of your mama- she was the one who helped me through this life each and every day."

"Daddy, you didn't tell me what happens to people when they die."

"Whenever that day comes, we go to heaven with God."

"Will *you* die daddy?"

"Sure I will. Everybody dies, I am no different from anyone else."

"I don't want you to die daddy," Ronnie said. Carson looked down at him as he began crying and remembered then how his hug was so strong, and he never wanted to let go.

"Buddy, when I am gone, you can't just stop living. You and I are so close, but leaving this world will be just as tough on me as it will be for you. Always remember though, I will be walking with The Lord, and I'll be with mama. Then one day, we three will be together, forever."

Builders across the deserted plains between the reservation and the city continued building in empty spaces, harboring some crazy hope of how people and jobs would come back to the area. It was after all, Washington D.C., the capital of the country and once quintessential example of a melting pot. Over many years, warm, dry winters followed summer droughts rendering the earth in and around the city to infertile dust. Only fifteen miles outside of the city, the reservation was built upon arbitrary peaks and valleys. The reservation was a place cursed since its inception. Because of the lack of rain, the people were not able to farm for themselves; fresh produce became rare and very expensive. The summer's oppressive heat rendered the inhabitants of the land limpid; it was a heat exposing every root and nerve, every sinew, doubt and the fact the people were unsettled and on the brink of losing hope. It was a heat that opened the bowels of the ground, exposing new veins whose blood had long since dried and turned to dust. The flood tried to take what was left of the soul of the land, and some say it took the collective strength of everyone to fight against it. Some here wondered, *"Why did it flood just here- why not the city?"* The deluge convinced some that if there was a God, he saw the people on the reservation as wicked. *"Why else would something like this occur to us?"* In truth, hope faded well before the waters came.

I, as a slave of The Specter of Evil, hated people for the nuisance they became and this life for me became a void only to be filled by Him- the one who could take my life into darkness because the light of the sun burned my eyes until there was no vision of love left in my heart.

The Specter orchestrated a maniacal climate of low self esteem and self-hatred which was the catalyst that actually backed the dwindling numbers into the reservation; adults and children alike killed themselves as well as each other over beefs, over images, over threats and over the rage they forced themselves to keep silent of when they woke up and found themselves hating themselves. Carson knew firsthand how they felt, but he knew how it was they themselves who had to realize jail cells, drugs, AIDS, the police and The Specter stood by patiently in the shadows of the reservation and beyond, waiting for them to commit sins which would bring them ever closer to oblivion. The Specter gained power by the day, the minute, the second, His hands stained crimson with the blood and desire of those who could and would have been great.

FOUR

VINCE HEARD THE players coming back in from practice through the halls as he sat in silence outside the Coach's office, waiting for his punishment. He knew for hitting another player with his helmet, there was a chance he would be thrown off the team.

"HILL!" Coach Turk yelled.

Vince came into his office and sat down. Coach Turk shuffled through some papers with his head down, and Vince was sure he was going to get kicked off the team. Vince was still not quite sure if he even trusted Coach Turk. He could have stopped the tussle between he and Mike at the cage long before it got out of hand.

"Son, once you step up your weight training program, nobody will be able to do to you what Mike did," Coach Turk said, smiling. *He's smiling. Why is he smiling?* "Look at Mike, he's the strongest player on our team. You are not the only one he has done that to. Hill, what I like about you is you got mad about it. You would not settle for just getting beat like that."

"Coach, I'm sorry I hit him, I…"

"Oh, don't worry about it Vince!" Coach said. "He'll be all right! You showed spirit out there today, I like that. One day, I'm gonna make an All-American outta you! I could make you the best player off any reservation!" He reached over and slapped Vince on the arm with a smile. "Let me tell you something son, you're a player with a lot of promise, and your father wants the best for you. You know son, your father David had a shot at playing in the big leagues. The man cares an awful lot for you, and from the moment you were born, he has been preparing you for playing sports. I remember when your father was much younger. He thought he was invincible. He was a great athlete, but his grades were not so good, and his attitude was even worse. Still, the schools overlooked all that, so long as he could catch and carry the football."

"He was good, huh, my dad?" Vince asked.

"Oh yeah, David was one of the best. He never really realized though, how many of the people who surrounded him- his teachers, his coaches, the college administration and any clingers who were ready to pounce only waited for him to succeed or fail in helping make money for the school."

"How did my dad feel about that, I mean, what could he do about it?"

"Feel? How he *felt* about anything was not important to the people who waited for him to make them money. David went wrong son by not realizing he could at least get an education. That's what I meant by saying he thought he was invincible. You can run son, but you can't run forever. Someday, you're gonna get old and when you do, you gotta have a life or you're gonna go crazy with shouldas and couldas. David had done well, up to the day of his tryout with a pro football team. That was the day when he could not break away from the drugs one of his well wishers had provided for him, free of charge. David lost track of time and snorted all night. The Devil was so happy he had grabbed up another one with his lies. As long as The Devil was by his side, David could make the football team without breaking a sweat, sign a contract without using a pen, catch a pass without havin' the ball thrown his way, break free from a defender without leavin' the line of scrimmage and for that matter have the love and respect of the crowds, the coaches and even the other players on his team without even taking a field or entering a stadium. With The Devil, he could have all those things sitting in his room, without even leaving his chair. He was lucky to make it back to the land of the living, but son, your father is determined not to let the same thing happen to you."

"I have been on this reservation my whole life, and I can remember from the time I was born, how my father put a ball in my hand," Vince said, shaking his head and suddenly realizing the true weight he carried. "He always used to joke, and call me 'his ticket outta here.' I never knew what he really meant by that. He used to talk a lot about movin' into the city.. into the city. He just wanted to get anywhere away from the dirt, the shacks, anywhere but here, and I was gonna take us."

"Go on home son, good work," Coach Turk said, with a hand on Vince's shoulder. *Good work?* Vince was certain Coach had a good tongue lashing waiting. He thought perhaps of being kicked off the team. Good work? Vince came away with the impression that the cheating he did out on the field was somehow okay.

So, if I hit him again, I'll get away with it? Nah, I'll get kicked off the team for sure this time. Sometimes I wish I didn't even have to deal with all this- the practicing, the sweating, the yelling, the hitting, the being made fun of. Sometimes, I just wanna be left alone.

Only the tip of the sun peeked out over the horizon of the reservation and as Vince walked home from practice, his father David sat at home half of him in darkness, the other half in the orange red light of dusk, believing the reservation to be his fate for his transgressions. The way he saw it, his son was gonna be his way out of there. He pushed Vince, in his words "to be his best." Once David broke a short distance away from The Specter's grip and became wrapped up in his own, he never looked for any kind of God, just a way to not hurt as much as he did before. David Hill came to the church every once in a while to hear Pastor Jenkins, when his guilt became too much for him to bear.

FIVE

As Carson sat within his modest flat, his color television brought in the one channel broadcast from the city. Old rhythm and blues songs he grew up with were used to advertise sodas, fried chicken, skinny white models in a lot of makeup, car insurance, shoes, jewelry and pills increasing sexual libido each and every day. Nothing was original anymore. It was as if people just stopped thinking, content with a small body of information they had acquired to yank ideas from. Among the adults on the reservation, it was murmured how a black man, young or old, never had a chance in a selfish, condescending world like the city in which money itself became The Lord. In fact, the adults on the reservation had many ready-made excuses all set to go, in case they ever had to answer for themselves and their lack of fight for their own well being and that of their children.

"Everthings rigged! What 'chu gon' do?"

"What's the use in even tryin?"

"I don't wanna go out there, they jus' gon' stab you in th' back!"

"It's a racist world, and I don' want no part of it!"

"Why should my kid have more than what I had growin' up?! That ain't fair!"

"I like it right here on the reservation, so at least I won't have ta' deal with them people out there! So what, I ain't rich, but, at least I can be left alone, and that's all I want anymore. Please, please just go far, far away and just leave me alone!"

Outside the small world of the reservation lied a long road leading to Washington D.C. Monday was the day for Carson's one drive per week and he usually spent it evangelizing on the streets of the city about the coming of Christ with Ronnie by his side. That day was the first he would go on without him. *I will go on without him.* He waited to leave the gate behind a bus picking up residents of the reservation and taking them to their jobs in the city. Most everyone in the more modern world outside of the reservation drove electric cars, but Carson had an old, gasoline driven Toyota, still hanging on for dear life. Each and every time he started it, the thing blew up in a cloud of black and white smoke. He tried to take advantage of any time he could get away from the reservation to evangelize, but with gas at ten dollars a gallon, he could not afford it. The long, flat road ran through a solemn wasteland of dead carcasses and wanderers seeking the truth; black nomads who were convinced of how the drugs they had obtained from within the city gates had shown them a better way of life and a better place than the reservation, perhaps even another reservation. The Specter of Evil was winning. *Lord, where are you?* Through the dirty windows of Carson's car, the wanderers saw his crisp, white collar and knew he was a representative of the church. Before he could get up to speed, they clamored around him.

"TAKE ME WITH YOU!"
"WHEN WILL GOD COME MY BROTHER?!"
"PRAY FOR ME!!"
"WILL WORK FOR FOOD!"
"THE DEVIL IS AMONG US!"

Some held signs of hope, while Carson suspected others just wanted the attention of anyone who would give it. As he drove the road, he remembered when the people prospered, worshipping God on a regular basis and he showered them with all the blessings they could carry and then some. The people misinterpreted those "blessings," coming to expect them in the form of silver, gold and the lotto. The people could never have it both ways. Precious metals became the focal point of their lives and among them, those who held the most of these things represented a closeness to God himself. Soon, it was the wealth they came to adore, and the deepening greed begat egomaniacal fools purporting to know the will of God and how they were willing to share it- for a price. As the burden of material things became greater by the day, their spirits waned and the land they walked on became a dry, desert place. Behind furs, gowns, jewelry and silk suits, the "religion peddlers" became entertainers on every channel appearing to relish the thought of becoming God's messengers on earth and many even gained a following. They actually "advertised" a relationship with God through the television, like prop up, cardboard brochures selling vacation destinations.

"For forty-nine ninety-five, plus tax, the cost of shipping and a small love offering fee with money you probably don't have but who cares, you too can establish a closer relationship with The Lord! Order Bishop So and So's tapes today! For The ultimate video experience, green ray discs are only sixty-nine ninety-five! Results may vary."

The Specter however, in several strange twists of fate, would not let them forget they were only human, even if the viewers could not immediately realize that. On the very same television screens which made the charlatans popular to the black masses, scandals, money laundering, extortion and extramarital affairs were just some of the foibles in which they dabbled and became destroyed in. *Oh well, nobody's perfect.* Once the people on the plains finally began catching on about how the people inside the box were only other people who really did not have The Lord's address, a part of the overall gross denial of the people was cut off. In other words, there was little left, outside of sports, left to entertain them while they waited on the second coming of Jesus. Flashy entertainment in the form of fancy rhetoric and sleight of hand had actually served to take their minds off the fact they hated each other. Besides, it was actually fun for many to bet on which of them might commit the first really serious faux pas. Disappearing and reappearing morals spoiled everything. Bored and without the "real entertainment" many on the plains took to heart, they began finding any excuse to kill each other, until there were few black faces left.

In the distance Carson saw the huge black gates preceding the city, where each resident or outsider coming in from the outside was greeted by armed guards. Above his head and throughout the perpetual clouds surrounding the dark, tall steel buildings, video billboards displayed dancing girls sporting wet lips as crimson as ripe cherries with supple bodies colored café au lait. Through the air were sounds of bells and whistles, sounds of women moaning, men moaning, vending to potential passing customers the thought of pleasure twenty four hours a day. Gigantic images of fifty and one hundred dollar bills bore talking faces, calling anyone hither who might listen. Whether for enlightenment or degradation, but mostly for degradation, the talking bills never held prejudice. The girls, the sounds, the painted faces- they were beasts and byproducts of beasts there to represent only what was tangible; sex and new drugs for many as the new God. The clean, manicured streets of the city lacked warmth, but were a masquerade for the city being a small society out of control. Once Carson was checked out by the guards, he was shown to a street corner.

"Where is the boy who usually accompanies you?" one guard asked. "Do you mind if we search your vehicle?"

"Don't bother searching, my son passed away," Carson replied without feeling.

"Come into no physical contact with anyone, or you will be forced to leave here!" one guard shouted. "Do you understand?!"

"Yeah! Yeah!" Carson replied.

Carson stood quietly apart from the sparse crowds surrounding him, holding a sign reading "God Is Coming." He stood alone contemplating life often, but after losing Ronnie, he could not remember such a time when he had ever felt so lonesome. Dark clouds passed over his head as people walked by with stoic, plastic faces, pale as the drying tide in what was left of the Potomac River at the bottom of the shore. Carson stood six foot four, two hundred and eighty five pounds among them, forcing people to walk around him. White women clutched their breasts as they passed, aghast solely by his presence. White men smaller in stature went by with their chests poked out, like little annoyed boys on playgrounds forever too small to be picked for any competitive game. Some went to work, dressed in the same drab grey suit with ties varying here and there. Some were off in leisure; many wore plaid or solid colored shorts exposing bare legs and sandals, along with similar blue t-shirts. Only the messages on the t-shirts varied. No one made eye contact with Carson because even with his social status among his own, he was an outcast in the city, a social anomaly, looked upon with hatred and dishonor as deranged. His presence to the hoards served only as a reminder of those black men in the past who willingly chose to remain ignorant of the future in a land of milk and honey, *their* land of milk and honey, as only the financially stable city dwellers themselves would have it. Those young black men who chose to comply with their new found opportunities in the land of promise, found themselves as infantrymen in the middle of wars representing big business when the United States economy was on the brink of complete collapse;

the total destruction and rebuilding of countries around the world had become the biggest business of all. In the process, many black men never lived long enough to see the land promised to them for their compliance, signing away on the dotted line of deceit their lives, praying to get through one more war- each one labeled "the war to end all wars." It was almost too late when they discovered "The war to end all wars" never existed; it was a catchy business phrase for those people in power who were all short of cash. In a state of pure ignorance and self-hatred, thinking ahead was too much for them to bear. The great flood actually provided what could have been a fresh start on the reservation, a whole new way of life, but the sparse number of black people left behind never learned gratitude even though their lives had been spared, and the air within the community quickly became again foul of mistrust, bravado and fear of one another.

Carson heard the wind floating past his face as he stood upon the streets of the empty white marble city that once flourished, wondering does a building still function as a building, even if there is never anyone inside of it? One thing was for sure, there were plenty of chances around to find out.

Carson stood within a womb of silence, protected from any disdain for the moment on that day away from the reservation, as he was no longer considered a real threat among the few whites passing by in the break of day, they being full aware of how his numbers had diminished. Everyone there was aware of how only certain ones from the reservation were allowed to leave beyond the gate- workers and clergymen. Through a brand new link fence with a "NO TRESSPASSING" sign off to the side, a children's soccer game was being played while many parents sat in the stands watching. One team was dressed in shining crimson jerseys, the other, royal blue. Parents cheered from the stands as one little blond haired boy almost scored a goal. Carson saw a bulldozer running over a nearby land which used to be the very neighborhood he grew up in. Long ago, when Carson was his son's age, the soccer field was a place where he waited for the girl of his dreams to come and play with him. He knew even then the playground was a place of quiet and solitude- strange words for a boy of twelve. That little girl turned what was then a forlorn field full of rusting metal play things into a place of hope. There Carson stood with hardened heart, believing there was some part of him coveting compassion, empathy, love- human emotions that could still be resurrected from the feldspar rocks and the distinct aroma of the reddish clay the bulldozer had unearthed. *What have I become? What is my purpose? Who am I? I feel for no one.* Through the new fence, the bulldozer snorted and growled. The apartment buildings where the girl he waited for used to live were already torn down and long gone. The next step was just to get rid of all the old playground stuff sitting covered in mud and black rust in the middle of the high weeds. The Jungle Jim covered in rust, the sliding board which no longer shined and the broken swings where Carson first met her.

I remember that day, one of the last days I would venture out to the swing set. Though the time was summer, and the sun still hovered over the horizon, I felt a chill over my body from sitting all day long. I knew from a distance, mother would have dinner ready soon.

I have been sitting here at this aging, forlorn swing set since early morning, only waiting. At times, I swing back and forth, and I even leave the swings every once in a while to go over to the sliding board which is right here beside me. Oh no, I am not going too far away. I have every intention of staying right here. Across the small dirt field against the high weeds, there are three red brick apartment buildings run by Old Mister Sheppard. Even in the light of the yellow red sun, all the windows appear gray, and I wonder which window she could be behind. Every day, Mister Sheppard sits under the giant tree by the hole in the fence where kids like me go in and out, and I don't know whether he thinks I did it or not. Even if he does think I am responsible, I am happy for the fact he leaves me alone to swing as long as I want. Perhaps he figures one child cannot possibly do a whole lot of damage. If Old Mister Sheppard has a change of heart, and tells me I can no longer come out here, my world will fall apart. I have played in the swings and on the sliding board every day for the past two weeks, while Old Mister Sheppard smokes his pipe under the giant tree. Each day for the past two weeks, when the sun finally goes down behind the grocery store on top of the hill, I walk by him on my way home as he continues to smoke his pipe. He wears an old fishing hat, and different colored short sleeve plaid shirts every day, and I see where his skin is all discolored from being burned one time, I guess really badly. The smoke from his pipe has an unusual smell, one I know Old Mister Sheppard by. He never looks at me when I come or go; he only slowly nods his head up and down in what I suppose is his own place of peace. He never once asked me why I wait in the swings every day after school, yet I suspect he knows why. He was out under the tree the day Tynette came out for the first time. My friend Nate, who lives on the other side of the hole in the fence in a house across the street, came out that day with me to swing. Many of the boys our age in the neighborhood never come to the playground- three pieces of play apparatus surrounded by high grass and weeds except for where our feet scratch the ground over and over under the swings revealing dirt and rocks- Nate and I knew that. Many of them our age around the neighborhood like to fight too much, within an endless makeshift proving ground. On that particular day, I believed Nate and I knew the playground was a place where we could find a little peace of our own. Peace is a funny word for a child, but I was sure Nate and I knew what it felt like, hence the alternative- fighting all the time for "fun." Nate and I were running about the playground when Tynette appeared out from one of the buildings- I'm pretty sure it was the building closest to me.

There are girls in my class at school, and some of them are even fun to look at, but when Tynette walked over and sat in the last swing in the row away from the two of us, I had never seen anything like her. She had long hair that was wavy, a different kind of dark, shining hair, but her skin was brown like mine. She had huge dark brown eyes- no other girl had eyes like that. Her eyes are not a thing I can explain to my parents, who are puzzled as to why I opt every day for this broken down playground at these fading apartment buildings up the street each day after school. As Tynette swang in the swing with no fear of it coming apart, she and Nate began talking almost immediately. I was afraid to say anything to her. I suppose I liked Nate because I could never see him putting on a pair of gloves in the middle of a field over the attention of a girl. In the midst of watching Tynette swing, I suddenly found myself wishing Nate would just go away, even though the way they got along was different, not like the way I envisioned myself with her. It had to be obvious to her that Nate and I were friends, but she did not say a word to me as the three of us went about playing in and around the swings. As she laughed with my friend, I took long glimpses of her when I thought she was not looking. Little did I know girls had eyes in the back of their heads. Her smile was enough to light up the world, and when she caught me staring at her, my heart dropped to my stomach when she smiled at me.

"Your name's Frankie?" she asked.

"Yeah," I mumbled.

"Well my name's Tynette!" she said in a proud way.

"Where you live?" she asked as she began swinging in the swing next to me.

"Up the street," I mumbled again. I took a deep breath and looked down at the ground, almost closing my eyes. "You got a boyfriend?"

"Why?"

"Nothin'."

"Why?" she asked again.

The way I kicked the ground and refused to look at her answered her question.

"We might only be around here for a little while," she sighed. "My dad moves a lot 'cause he's in the Army. I have to start at a new school Monday, and I don't know why because I'm just gonna have to move a-gain!"

Nate slid on the sliding board a short distance away, while Tynette's swing slowed down and came to a halt. I looked over at her as she looked down at the ground, shuffling rocks on the ground underneath her with her feet. For a moment, it seemed like she was going to cry. And then in the midst of really, really wishing Nate would go home, something happened.

Nate got tired, and dirty, and began walking across the street to his home. As he made his way down the path, past Mister Sheppard and through the shortcut hole in the apartment complex fence created through impatience, I realized she and I were alone. There was Tynette, still sitting still in the swing, with me in the one beside her. I knew the swing set was old, but as if by instinct, or fear or both, I began swinging fast and high. I just wanted to show her how high I could get in the old thing. She finally looked up at me.

"Frankie, Frankie, I wanna get that high too!"

I stopped the swing on a dime over the rocks, ran around behind her and began pushing her by placing my hands firmly on her back. Every time I touched her, it registered in my mind that she felt different. Every time she came toward me, and I would have to touch her, I marveled at the fact that she was unlike anything I had ever encountered, I mean, she was completely different from my sisters when we fought. My sisters always wear those little glass balls in their hair that dangle at the end of their pigtails to keep them from coming apart and so did Tynette, but in her hair I noticed their actual aesthetic value. She even smelled different, like something wonderful. It could have been that Sulfur Eight hair stuff from the drug store my mother used sometimes for all I knew. I found myself wanting to touch her. She did not want to go too high after all, and when she achieved a steady pace, she began talking to me again. I like listening to her talk. Once she had managed to keep her own rhythm going, I got back in the swing next to her and began going back and forth again. Soon in the midst of talking, we both lost all momentum and ended up only sitting with the two swings twisted toward one another. As she talked about some of the places she had been, I saw she was really an okay girl.

The light of the day began fading as I smelled the combination of many different home cooking aromas from out of the windows of the apartment building, and I guessed my own dinner was probably about to be put on the table at home. There was an excellent chance of my parents punishing me for not being home at the time they served dinner. Tynette and I twisted back and forth, and side to side as we talked, and at one long point, we began laughing as our legs became wrapped together, she in a dress. We both knew full well we had to be home as the light of the day was almost gone, but there were five or six seconds when we looked into each other's eyes and said nothing at all. I had never felt like that before.

I looked down at the rocks beneath our feet just to not stare into her eyes anymore. It was too much for me. I did not know what more to say to her. I guessed then how there were things people knew without the benefit of being told. It was a fact for example, that my parents were wondering where in the world I was, and it was a fact Nate was my friend, yeah, and it was also a fact this girl was the most beautiful thing I had ever seen. Our heads touched as the swings we sat in were twisted beyond the belief of any living child and then I kissed her. I actually kissed the girl. That was the moment the forlorn apartment complex playground with a field full of dirt and weeds needing a lawnmower became my gigantic, magical reason for living, apart from eating sweets.

Sometimes I count the number of rocks laying in the sand at my feet as I wait for Tynette. When I am not counting rocks, I look out into all the high grass and weeds in the neglected field and imagine her running out from behind the building. She will be so glad to see me, and she knows how long I have been waiting. I snap out of my dream every so often to see only the weeds. Mister Sheppard is way too old to cut the grass, but seeing him sit under the tree all day, I think the grass is the last thing on his mind. I read the new white signs with bold black letters poked into the ground all around the apartment complex saying the property is for "lease." I do not understand what "lease" means, but I think someone might be looking for a reason to tear down this rusted old swing set and sliding board. I hope every time Old Mister Sheppard sits out under the tree and sees me sitting in the swing, or sliding down the board, it might give him the idea that someone actually likes it out here.

I have a letter in my pocket, that I wrote just for her;

Dear Tynette

Please give me a chance
to be your boyfriend

you are so cute
and I think I love you

I'll give you all my money
And a lot of candy
For another kiss

Frankie

To tell the truth, I have nearly lost all hope because I think she moved away. I just want to swing and wait, one more time. I know my parents were puzzled when I left home early- on a day of no school. I said nothing that would lend them information toward my state of mind, or where I was going. I think they know anyway.

Hours have passed, but the Sun still hovers over my head. Regardless of how long I wait, I know that as long as the sun is in the sky, I have a chance.

There are times when waiting in this swing and sliding down the sliding board is absolute torture, even for someone as young as me. I try looking up into people's windows sometimes from down here, through their curtains and blinds. I can hear, from a short distance away on the other side of the building, how the people in my neighborhood are at it again. I hear a crowd gathering by the creek where the older boys like to put on boxing gloves and fight all day. I do not much care about them, or how much blood there is over there for sport. So much blood, and everyone over there likes it that way. I don't know how my parents put up with living here. If I was all grown up, I would take Tynette and leave this place far behind. Where could we go to be away from all this? Once, I stood in the crowd and watched as a new boy tried to take on the whole neighborhood while people yelled and screamed around him. As he took on boy after boy, I saw a look on his face that he thought he had something to prove to everyone. Dust rose higher and higher into the air with fight after fight and I swear, I could not understand the point, or, what I was even doing there. So I left, amid people pushing and shoving one another to get closer to the fray.

As he looked through the fence at the soccer game, Carson felt something; a hostile presence. Slowly, he turned to see a small horde of city dwellers, mostly whites, who had gathered nearby to stare at him. There were young, as well as old in the small throng, and their postures all shared a stance of disdain, of hostility upon their ashen presence.

"You're *black*," a child who stood by her mother said. Her curly blonde locks were almost white. The expression on her plastic face was one of perfect scorn, schooled in the subtle nuances of hate. That expression was identical on all their faces. Carson read and judged their possible intent and caught wind of an odor, a stench, permeating the air. At first it was the smell of old dirt, and then like fresh red clay just unearthed. Then, quickly the odor turned- like a plague of worms over something long dead, or an entire culture resigning itself to a great death. Through buildings and streets overhead, through others standing and walking nearby and down past where he stood, Carson saw it- coming toward him as a light mist. He reasoned it to be a stink of prejudice, perhaps a bouquet of warning. Carson realized the streets he stood on were no longer his home and he actually longed for the reservation. The little blond girl stood holding her mother's hand and once she made her comment, Carson knew she had her mother's approval to harass him because there was no effort to rein in her mouth.

"Yes, you're very perceptive," Carson replied.

"What are you doing here?" the girl asked.

"What am I doing here? What are you- a puppet or something, speaking for these people around you who have their hands up your little wooden back that cannot speak for themselves? Run along!" He found himself getting angry and prayed for calm.

"You heard her," the mother finally said. "What *are* you doing here?"

"Why, to tell you God is coming- can't you read the sign?" *Can't you read the sign?*

"We already know he is coming."

"Uh-huh!" Carson shot back. "Your anger and prejudice toward anyone not like you has turned inward, which by the way, equals depression. Not from where I stand you don't!"

"And whom might you be?" she asked, sneering.

"A man who used to live right here, and one who has just as much right to be here as any of you!" Carson replied hastily.

"If that were true, you would still be living here," a man within the crowd replied. "You don't live here anymore. This is *our* home."

"No- this is God's home- you're just borrowing it for the time being!" Carson spat back.

"Like you're borrowing the reservation?" another said. "Why don't you go back there- we don't like your kind here."

"My *kind*- what *kind* are you? Oh wait, don't tell me- you're mental giants! You suffer from depression and a lack of sun, and you believe in nothing outside of money, but you're mental giants! I go where my God tells me to go- not you!

What, you think I'm some kind of Uncle Tom or something, where I just have to be around the likes of you to make me feel good about myself? This is actually improper for me to say, but why don't you go back to the hell you're already in, and tell everyone here I said so!"

"I think your God should lead you home now blackie!"

"Hmm, gotta say I could see that coming," Carson said with his anger rising, "but that fake Jedi mind stuff you got out of old comic books only work on the weak minded- like you. You'll have to come a lot better than that!"

"Blackie! Blackie! Blackie!!" They all shouted in unison. The little child led them. Looking through the fence, the place of a cherished memory, there were even people on the other side who had been watching the confrontation, chanting the slur. Looking into the face of hate, Carson turned, adjusted his sign, and stood still.

SIX

"WE'VE GOT THE VICTORY! C'mon and put
your hands together for The Lord! Has he not
been good to you?" Pastor Jenkins shouted upon a
pulpit made up of wooden boxes strewn together.
Behind the makeshift pulpit on which he stood
was a picture of a white, slightly tanned Jesus
Christ whose face was free from any spots or
blemishes. He bore a perfect smile of the whitest
teeth, along with shining, flaxen hair. Mounted
upon a large piece of plywood, the picture itself
looked like a still from a toothpaste or shampoo
commercial, but its surface was spotted with some
water residue from the flood. "Stand on your feet
and give him some praise!"

A shield of thick glass protected the small
choir made up of young girls. Their uneven voices
indicated their best effort, donned in brown paper
bag robes with crosses painted on them with water
colors. A young, fair skinned girl played a drum

set behind Pastor Jenkins. Pastor Jenkins knew the people in front of him had been waiting and waiting on God to come and pass judgment upon those who harmed them, but no one had harmed them as much as they had harmed themselves. Over the years of working and toiling for a living, the memories of the people had been cursed with drinking, smoking and forgetting their strengths, as well as who they served. For some, the clothes they stood in were all they had left after the flood. Each Sunday, the people collected at The Baptist Church of The Reservation to wait in seated positions for solutions to their problems. Carson sat in the front pew reserved for Deacons, which was the only row of pews within the glass. The church was small in leadership; besides Pastor Jenkins, Carson, was one of four Deacons. There was no floor in the church, only the bare, sienna dirt and sometimes mud of the earth and weeds. The congregation swelled behind Carson, pounding against the glass and marking graffiti on the naked cinder block walls. Many of them shouted with clenched fists, some threw eggs and some only sat silent within the chaos watching and wondering. The mouths of the choir moved, but Carson could no longer hear them over the uprising of the congregation. *Will God really come back for us?* Over the years, over its fifteen years of existence, The Baptist Church of the Reservation on Sundays became a social gathering place first and not necessarily a house of religious worship. On the reservation, it was one of the last remaining vestiges of entertainment, besides the casino, and the congregation showed its pleasure or displeasure in no uncertain terms, like a gong show. Beside Carson was an empty space where his son used to sit and he remembered how he always looked up to him. At that moment, he remembered a conversation they once had.

"How did I shoot the ball today daddy?" Ronnie asked.

"You shot great buddy, you always do," Carson replied, rubbing his son's head.

"Daddy do you want me to grow up to be a ball player?"

"You can grow up to be what you want to be Ronnie, so long as what you do is legal under God."

"I don't wanna go to jail, daddy!"

Carson laughed. "I know you don't little one. One thing I want you to understand is you can do whatever you want. You're a smart little guy and, well, you're the best!"

"Thank you daddy," he replied. "Daddy?"

"Yeah?"

"You're the best daddy too. I love you daddy."

The other Deacons were kind enough to already reserve a place on the row for Ronnie with a plaque, and as Carson gazed at the shining gold plate beside him, he continued to sit in the pew, saying nothing, looking at no one, not clapping, but in wonder at the very idea of his *son* waiting for *him*, along with his mama. Carson saw the number of people on the other side of the glass screaming, some cursing and some still praising God, despite many of their ruined lives. Though they bellowed at the top of their voices, he heard none of them, because he simply did not want to. Carson knew they too had lost loved ones, besides material things and perhaps even dreams. On some of the days he stood outside the ragged gate of the reservation looking in, he wondered how the people within were not completely stripped of spirit, and everything that went with it. Carson had stopped by the church on his way home expecting no one there, but found a house full of people. *At least they are here, at least they still have a chance at truly living.*

Carson felt the unruly congregation making its way toward the glass behind him, once Pastor Jenkins took a step back within the pulpit, looking as if a tidal wave was about to hit him. Through the light overhead and just behind him, Carson noticed many smeared fingerprints of whole hands upon the surface of the glass and perhaps upon his own grief. From his place in the pulpit, Pastor Jenkins nodded toward Carson. A makeshift band played on in the crowd beyond the glass, beating on plastic containers as if they were conga drums in an attempt to overwhelm the sound of the young girls in the choir. Pastor Jenkins threw his hands up toward the window at the darkening sky outside above the church.

"Never give up faith people!" he screamed. "God will never give up on you! We will wait, and be of good courage! Press! Let us press on until the end! Your will be done my Lord! Raise your hands if you still believe in The Lord! Raise your hands to show that you still believe in the Lord! I too have lost everything, but those were just material things and I will never put my faith in material things that will wither away in time! You can have the Lord for always! He has given us a second chance, so count it all joy! I will wait on you Lord, to see what the end will be! We're still here and we love you! Despite all that has happened, we're still here! We're still here!!!"

At that moment, many behind the glass became consumed by a spirit of good will that flowed through the church and began dancing through the pews of folding chairs. There were many angry non-believers who pelted the glass with eggs and drinks every chance they got and some even held up signs of protest, proclaiming how Pastor Jenkins was lying and that God really did not exist. When he looked back to view the faction of unrest, Carson saw The Specter standing among them. Yes, even in the house of God, The

Specter had gained entry; the people's ignorance of their past plight serving as his invitation. Even among the people who held out hope, the oily, distorted fingerprints covering the glass were silent indicators of complete desperation.

Rain began falling on Carson's way to church from the city. Once he headed for home, it grew heavy, with dark, shining water running like crude oil down muddy, battered roads. Dark figures stood on corners like chess pieces- pawns- in relationship to one another. Though the rain was heavy, it was nothing compared to the destruction the area endured from the flood. In truth, the rain felt merciful to Carson; as if God had actually eased his wrath upon the plains. A guard from the reservation's gate began approaching as Carson began pulling out his identification within the car.

"Aw, no need, Deacon," he said through the pouring rain with a wave of his hand, "I just came out to say hi- there's your parking spot over there. Sorry 'bout your son. Try to have a good night!"

"Thanks."

Carson never wanted the teenagers who sought refuge on the street away from their drinking, gambling parents to see him with any privilege outside of his own car which was falling apart. As much as he wanted to help them with a magic word of some sort, many of them brandished the fact of how they did not want help from anyone, opting instead for a life of open air adventures consisting of drinking, drugging and dodging the scant police force. Carson walked through the liquid night without an umbrella as silhouetted figures on both sides of the road yinged and yanged, many gesturing with their hands going haywire to make a point like all the days of their lives on the reservation clouded with self-destructive emotions. The odor of raw sewage permeated the humid air, amid the drainage systems that had not recovered from the flood, but to Carson, it was the perfume of home. The water running past his feet contained the dirt and mud of memories for some and complete nightmares for some others. The tired, pain-riddled shanties appeared beautiful under the falling water of the night sky. *This is my home now, within the dying spirit of the black world.* A man sat on a public bench just ahead, an elderly man who called himself Leslie. His dark wrinkled face bore white stubble from having not shaved in days. He wore a lopsided, sopping wet blonde wig and a mini skirt revealing thin, broken, hairy legs. He wore no socks, only a pair of cheap, soiled running shoes he found at a charity. He sat and waited, be it in a shrouding rain or under a revealing sun. In the dark of night, he waited, *knowing* there was a demand for his homosexual company, no matter how miserable doing tricks made him.

"Here Leslie, when you're tired, take a look at this card," Carson said. "It has a prayer on it- I'm not asking you to come to church or any place you don't want to go, I'm just saying look at it sometime when you're alone and you need comfort. It will help you."

"I'm alone now," he said in a deep, feminine voice, wiping the drenched blond strands from his worn eyes. "You wanna sit with me?"

"No, I need rest," Carson said wearily, looking skyward to let the rain wash his face. "Besides, I don't wanna see you solicit people for sex when you could be doing something else, something other than this."

"Suit yo-self," he said, turning his head and crossing his legs.

The muddy bench was all Leslie knew and all he cared to know. Before the flood, he had become intimate with a bench somewhere else that allowed him to transgress. Perhaps a byproduct of the flood's destructive purpose *was* to expose as well as wash away. As Carson continued walking, he looked across the street at a man named Harold who, in his constant drunken state, knew everything there was to know about God. *Instant, liquid knowledge that will disappear with a crash.* Carson knew he could ask Harold about Judaism, Hinduism, Christianity, Islam, taxes or anything else on his mind, including why Jesus had not come back yet, and he could tell all.

He stood with a group of young boys who sold drugs on the side of the road, begging for their product because he had no money. Lip service. There was little left of what used to be the usual stuff; marijuana died out decades ago for people in search of a faster way to get high. Kids, and adults who misled them, were into inhaling from aerosol cans, along with smoking a new "super" form of cocaine, burning and sniffing household cleansers, plastics, glue and some prescription drug of the future which sped up their libidos. The trouble was many of them had thrown their "futures" in the trash, not ever willing to be part of any society, white or otherwise, particularly one in which their parents never bothered to learn a language of love. Carson supposed there would always be a demand among many people for a means to escape their lives, even on a temporary basis. *If the people of the reservation did not like where they were living, they could have just said so and done something about it.*

Carson walked to his flat, wondering what his purpose in life really was, realizing he was almost sixty years old and he still really did not know how to take care of himself. *How then can I care for others? Is my reason for living only to minister to the sick and dying?* Carson wondered was his purpose to stand up in the middle of the reservation, perhaps in a driving rainstorm, for a higher ideal among people who were seduced by brilliant colors and the lure of money? Was it to stand among people who had convinced themselves of being have-nots and that their very blackness lent itself to sacrilege? Carson thought one option was to walk away and turn his back in silence while the children of the reservation willingly died- throwing their hands up for their turns like enthusiastic elementary students who were certain of how three came after two- instead of carving out a piece of dignity in what they saw as a corrupt world. Carson feared the youth were perhaps never given credit for what they saw as the truth, only judged for their destructive actions which they learned from the adults before them. Perhaps they sensed how outside the ragged gate and beyond, it was only a world of who had money and who did not. *No money, no honey, no matter who you are, or who you think you are.* In other words, in their view, cash determined who had any proximity at all to The Lord or maybe even a pile of cash might be able to buy a stay from certain execution of his wrath.

Upon opening the door to his place, the first thing Carson saw was a basketball. He looked over in a corner at another ball, and then saw a pair of Ronnie's shoes. Carson went to his bathroom, and looked into a mirror, letting out a sigh at the sight of his brown bearded face covered with tears that became older before his eyes under a weak fluorescent light overhead. White hairs had crept up through his dark brown hair as well as the hair on his face, and it was like he was seeing them for the very first time. Carson looked down at his hands, took a bar of soap, and began washing them. He washed them again, and again, and again. Every time he washed the white lather off them with water, they remained black. He wanted to pour bleach on them, to see if they would change color, perhaps to a color which did not bring with it so much misfortune. He scrubbed at them, over and over until they began to bleed. After sixty years, after battling with The Specter of Evil years ago, after seeing the deaths of his wife and son, his entire life came down to a moment of silence in front of a bathroom mirror. Trouble was upon his door again. *Am I truly a man of faith?* Carson realized his skin color would never change. He picked up the basketball, and laid down on his bed. He was not hungry. Carson curled up, and closed his eyes, still soaking from the rain.

"Hey Blackie! Blackie! Blackie!! Blackie! Blackie! Blackie! Blackie! BLACKIE!!!!"

Aw, c'mon man, who woke you up today, and who got you through today? Didn't The Lord put you in your right mind, and send you on your way this morning? Never mind that mob. Rain or shine, wasn't it a beautiful day? Great. Now you know, some people did not live to see the light of day, but you did. Just like you thought, God placed his finger of love on you. So what happened then, to the ones who did not live to see daylight? Did God not put his finger of love upon them? Are you thinking those people are better off dead? Are you thinking you've been chosen to do something? What about so many of these people walking around in the land of the living who are already dead? Heck, who knows- you just gotta concentrate on not being one of 'em. I know what you're thinking now; if you do go to heaven, you're wondering will you get there in your present state of mind because you've got a lot of questions. For example, how come everybody in church always shout hallelujah and amen at the thought of coming to live with God, but when it's really time to go, they fight like the devil with doctors in hospitals and arm themselves with a boatload of prayers begging Him to allow them more time on earth? I know it might seem to you no one really wants to leave. Hmmm. When you get right down to it though, even I gotta ask what is it that we're so reluctant to leave behind?

SEVEN

IT WAS DURING the seventh day of school within the overcrowded, long and winding hallways of Redemption High School, a building full of open air classrooms where students of the reservation could hear exactly what other students in other rooms were *thinking*. For some in the school, the hallways were only a means to get to class. For others like Vince Hill, the halls were trouble, full of many young drones who carried drugs, mayhem and unknown to him, fresh souls to The Specter of Evil himself. For Vince, the halls were a way to death, plain and simple and he avoided being in them as much as possible. So many vacant stares, only few about the business of school, including some teachers. During that seventh day, at 8:20 AM, the passageways were crowded and absent of light while profanity filled the air. Drugs were exchanged. Cigarettes were given out. Drinks were exchanged and images were secured through loud arguing and fighting. What occurred between the students that day were moments of silence within the cacophony which was the sound of their voices, all defiant, full of venom, full of angst. Within those moments of silence, time stood still, as if their very actions came to a halt. That morning, those moments revealed a fear which only comes with the transition of pubescence into adulthood. Who were they? Where were they going? What was within the outside world that was even worth living for? Being honest with oneself was never a easy thing at that age or any age, but only those who were honest with themselves would even begin to approach the answer to those questions. The rest would remain in limbo, their lives trapped within a cocoon of fear that might never break, no matter the season. The halls were a place tucked within the recesses of time, a scene ever repeating itself, while parents remained aloof, demanding only to be entertained on Sundays at church. When the government built Redemption, they thought it would be big enough to suit all the students' needs. Over time, nomads from other parts were let in, yet the government felt no need to build another facility. The hallways created a counterculture among the youth involving self-destruction and noncompliance. *Son, what it mean son, to be young and restless? Destroying our places of prosperity and or privilege, turning the light of day into the blurred picture inside our malnourished minds; the huge ghetto which has come to light based on our lack of direction handed to us by our parents who, by a roll of the dice, never cared how they were unaware that they were unaware of not having the tools to equip us? All we knew or even remembered was the brochure they found of the reservation with artists' renderings of happy black adults and their children playing with a hedge of protection around them in the form of a white picket fence, and the pictures of those children gave us the idea that we had a chance to succeed outside the gate. Back then, we stood in the halls of school and laughed at the idea of self-esteem being just a game, huh man? Well.. ain't it?!*

To any teacher who looked outside his own overcrowded door, he saw children struggling mightily to protect themselves from a world of hurt; a place where inmates ran the "asylum." It was up to teachers to not leave any child behind mentally or physically, even if they wanted to be left behind. Within the mind of many of the children left on the reservation, it was not their intention to come to a class to get "good grades" to be a part of a world where they felt they were not included. They believed in two avenues for them in the outside world- mayhem and sports- football or basketball, with the hope of reaching a professional level. Mayhem, in the form of selling drugs. Over the years, sports leagues became corrupt when players found out they could actually make more money by cheating. A missed shot here, a fumble there, an errant swing of the bat, undetectable performance enhancing drugs and no one was the wiser. Despite the public suspicion over sports leagues existing in that state for years no one seemed to care until it was exposed how some referees were involved in organized crime, and had been gambling on the outcome of games. Well, that was the last straw. The white public was the only one who could actually afford to go to the games anymore anyway. Those people in the cities had donned themselves in memorabilia and paraphernalia of their favorite teams for years. They lived and died for every Sunday or Monday or Saturday or Thursday or any other day ending in y when games were aired on television. They were slow to believe any of it. Even the city dwellers however in their denial, could not ignore one thing; the leagues were becoming more "black" by the year, versus the fact they saw black people nowhere else outside of menial jobs in the city and on television for committing crimes. Young black men on the reservation were willingly bred and raised for the sports arenas, but those same young black men also represented the idea of being against the "white land of milk and honey," terrorizing any idea of community- even within their own- by influencing the young behind them to be alienating and unabashedly selfish.

Suddenly, as students continued to meander back and forth in the halls, a voice came over the intercom above their heads, the same automated one which came on every morning: *"Ladies and Gentlemen, please hurry to your classes, in the interest of learning. We know what looms outside these doors; a broken down reservation after the flood, filled with what might be the remnants of dreams. Your dreams. We can build anew. You have a decision to make- a decision to believe. If you decide not to get your education, you will join those people outside who have no direction- instead of being free to create, to dream, to simply make a life for yourself. It makes no difference really where you live, you can create a picture of beauty or chaos that you want to live in within your own mind. Do you understand? Move expeditiously to your rooms to greet another day of learning; a day in which you can become a better person."*

Vince looked around the classroom. A few of the students around him were asleep, others held blank stares upon their faces, chewing gum. And then, two or three of them looked as if they had actually heard every word the intercom said. *Welcome, to the world.*

Vince usually stayed awake for Geometry class, though he only heard half of what Mrs. Gabby ever said. He managed to stay awake because he could never take his eyes off Olivia Henry, a girl who was new to the school who sat in front of him. Day after day in those days at the start of the school year, Vince wondered how to let her know she was the most beautiful thing he had ever seen. Judging from the silver cross she wore around her neck, Vince guessed Olivia was a girl whose family was fond of the church. By her silent demeanor, Vince judged she was not the kind of girl who cussed, or smoked cigarettes out front of the school before, during and after classes like so many others did. Vince sometimes wore his football jersey in the hope she might notice him. She never budged. Vince gathered she did not feel one way or another about football or sports in general. In fact, if he had to guess, he would have said she actually disapproved of football because of the dirt, the fighting and the overall noise. Vince was taken by her the first time she came into class, which was the second day of school. She was from out of town, the New York City area in fact.

"Miss Henry is from where, New York City?" Miss Gabby asked.

"Yes ma'am, New York City," she responded in the sweetest voice, standing in the doorway.

The class was unimpressed, except Vince.

She came into the class and took the empty seat in right in front of Vince. She was slender and fair-skinned, with long, dark brown hair, and large brown eyes. She was dressed in a modest red dress with simple flat red shoes. She wore a pair of thick rimmed glasses, restraining her looks to the casual, passing eye. Vince saw right through them however, to her clear skin and her peaceful, upright posture.

Geometry class was the only one Olivia and Vince shared, and the moment she walked into it, it became his favorite class.

"Mister Hill!" Miss Gabby called. "Could you take your eyes off Miss Henry for just a second, and come up to the front of the class and demonstrate for us how to do a proof of an isosceles triangle?"

Everyone turned to look at Vince, and he just wanted to hide. Everyone turned except Olivia. She sat with her head down, blushing. Vince had been in his own private world admiring her, day after day. He was hesitant of Olivia finding out he was enamored of her by way of Miss Gabby's mouth, but at least she knew. Vince liked everything about her; the way she came into class everyday carrying her books close to her chest, her quiet manner, never mind the fact she was new, and that she wore a dress every single day.

Vince stood exposed for all the class, and Olivia, to see.

"Well, Mister Hill, what are you waiting for?" Miss Gabby called.

"Yes, ma'am," Vince responded. He got up, and walked past Olivia, careful not to let her see how really embarrassed he was. The quick glimpse he did get of her as he walked by did not reveal her face, as she looked away and down toward the papers on her desk. Vince picked up the chalk from the blackboard and just stood there, not even remembering the question.

"An isosceles triangle, Mister Hill?"

Vince hated geometry. Between football practice, and English class, history class and other classes, geometry was his absolute last priority. Vince was already failing the class, and did not remember cracking the book once at home since Olivia came into the room, opting instead to imagine what it would be like to spend time with her.

Vince stood in front of the class, not knowing the first thing of what Miss Gabby was talking about.

"That's what I thought Mister Hill!" Miss Gabby said. "You may take your seat now!"

Vince turned away from the blackboard, intent not to let Olivia see his face. *That's what I thought Mister Hill!* At that moment, he wished she could know he was not some dummy. That was the only important thing to him- whatever Olivia was thinking. He did not care about the rest of the class, just her. Though she never turned around, she knew he liked her, feeling the heat of his gaze upon her shining hair, no thanks to Miss Big Mouth Gabby. Vince took his seat behind her, already sensing how most of the class was shaking their heads as if to say, "another dumb football player, what else is new?" So what.

When class was over, Olivia stood up and Vince's hand almost touched her hair.

"Mister Hill, will you come up front please?" Miss Gabby called.

"Yes, ma'am," Vince responded.

"I hate geometry too," Olivia turned to Vince and said, with a smile.

"*Ohmigod!*" Vince whispered.

"Mister HILL!"

"Uh, yes, yes ma'am!"

"Mister Hill, what is your problem in my class?" Miss Gabby asked. "It's not like this work is the hardest stuff in the world, You're just not paying attention!"

"Yes ma'am, I'm sorry!"

"This week, I'm going to have to declare you ineligible for your football game! You're getting an 'F' in my class this week!"

"Yes ma'am," Vince replied, overjoyed.

"You find all that good news do you Mister Hill?"

"She smiled at me."

"I beg your pardon?"

Vince started out the door. "She smiled at me before she walked out of the room. And now she knows I like her, thanks Miss Gabby!"

"You young people are nuts!" she called after him.

Vince knew where Olivia's locker was, and just "happened" to stroll by during the change of class and caught her in the hallway. She smiled again. Vince had put on one of his stinking practice jerseys to impress her. "Hi, I'm Vince."

"Hello, I'm Olivia," she said, looking down and barely able to contain a smile.

"You are the most beautiful girl I have ever seen," Vince blurted.

"Thanks," she said, almost laughing.

"You hate geometry too, huh?"

"Yes, and I felt really bad for you when you were in front of the class. What's that *smell*?"

"I want you to know what she said was true, you know, about me staring at you, though I know I can't blame you for the bad grade I got in her class this week."

"That's good," she said, holding her hand to her nose.

"Olivia, have you made any friends yet?"

"Not really," she said, with a wave of her hand. "I've just been here two weeks."

"You can have lunch with me every day if you want!"

She laughed. "I'll think about having lunch with you today Vince, that's what you mean, right?"

"No, I mean every day. Every single day."

"Would you do me a favor?" she asked.

"Anything, any- any-thing, you just name it, whatever it is, just name it!" Vince pleaded.

"Would you not wear this jersey? It stinks."

Olivia and Vince talked in a quiet corner beside the rising and falling voices eating and joking in the vast cafeteria, away from the loud thugs who had a whole world to prove themselves to just so they could be left alone, or just not picked on like the rest. Olivia told of what it was like growing up in New York, a city which according to her, seemed crowded. She and her mother came from a poor section of the city, a part where all black people lived. There was no reservation up there yet, with that idea being in the works because of the growing crimes the young blacks committed against whites.

As Olivia talked, there was a glow from her like no one Vince had ever known. Olivia had no brothers or sisters, and she and her mom lived together in an apartment across the reservation. Olivia and her mother were religious people, often going to the church three or four times in one week. If there were no services, they went to see if they could help out with something. While Olivia talked about how much she loved God, and how He was the reason for everything good in her life, a certain peace was about her very being, if it was possible for someone so young. She was even convinced of how God had sent Vince to her and that their paths were destined to cross.

EIGHT

Mister and Mrs. Trotter lived across the reservation, on the other side- the very edge of the government property that might not be considered "bad," or at least, they and a few others living around them kept trying over the years to decorate their humble abodes by planting grass seed around them, hoping for a yard of green which would at least represent some semblance of the lives they had before. In the prosperous old days, Henry Trotter was a corporate investor who did quite well. She was the adoring housewife who had dinner waiting for his return from work each and every night. He was a proud man who happily provided for his wife, and in those prosperous old days, there was jewelry, cars, and within him, an element of recklessness. One night during a holiday season, he attended an office party with his co-workers during the peak of the company's prosperity. That same night, he became a slave of The Specter of Evil, inhaling the new drug every chance he got. Henry Trotter, a proud man, stood in a bathroom alone in front of a mirror feeling his new found power. He believed he had helped the company to forge ahead, but he was passed over for promotions he felt he should have gotten. On the drug, he felt promoted, powerful, desirable. The feeling lasted for a few minutes, then he began to hear things around him as it wore off. Conversations penetrated walls and through his head that may or may not have been about him. He heard the sounds of crows outside on that humid December night, feasting on what was left of a deer carcass in a field outside the building. As the drug wore off, he no longer wanted to look at himself in the mirror anymore; he no longer wanted to be The Man. He only wanted to be left alone, until he could figure out a way to get more, with The Specter looking on, pleased he had brought someone else into his fold of darkness with so little effort and so little resistance. Mr. Trotter succeeded for a short time in keeping his transgressions a secret, until his appearance faltered; gone were the bright eyes revealing an intelligence that knew how not to tread on others while making its point. There was weight loss and suddenly, to Mrs. Trotter, the lines of her husband were not as crisp upon his person as he left out the door for work, rather, he wore the look of a desperate man, one who began shrugging off the responsibilities and values he himself had built as easily as lint began gathering on his sweaters. For as long as the grass would not grow on the infertile land of the reservation, Mister Trotter was saved from the cumbersome chore of having to take care of it during his freefall, therefore not having to reveal his impending neglect. In other words, if his yard was the only one with dying grass, the nosy neighbors might figure something was amiss. Mister Trotter was a man before not bad to look at, with manicured hair and nails, always fresh clothing and even toned brown skin. Once he met The Specter, it was Mrs. Trotter within the house and out of sight who suffered all the neglect she could handle. The Specter sensed the weakness in her husband and had been beckoning him, urging him to give in to his fantasies of what he thought he could have been- a jetsetter attending wild parties with beautiful women of all colors who saw in him new inroads of gluttony and perhaps spontaneity. In reality, the "parties" he envisioned ended up to be only tense paranoid moments from the effects of the drugs with any female he thought he actually convinced to join him; they were in reality women of the night who worked as lures for The Specter- stale eye candy that- in his mind- softened the blow of his fall from grace.

Mrs. Trotter was a beautiful woman who believed in the idea of loving one man, and she believed she had found that man in her husband, always remembering the time he swept her off her feet at all places, a church she visited with a friend. She was brought up in the church and her parents had her believe it was a great place to find Mister Right. He, at the advice of a friend attended church that day because he was told it was a great place to find a girl he could one day maybe "take home." From the time the two of them met, he always made her laugh and she was impressed by the fact he had a good job and made good money. She suspected nothing when he came home many a late night, even though he always said the same thing:

"Oh, honey, I had a late night. I'm sorry, I should have called, I just got so caught up in the work- we have deadlines to meet," he said with bloodshot eyes and a strange odor about him, like sweet candy in a smoldering fire.

"Baby, I was so worried, I'm just glad to know you're okay!" she sighed.

Perhaps she suspected something in the beginning; but nothing compared to the reality of her husband becoming enslaved by a renegade higher power. Mr. Henry Trotter had taken time out of his schedule to listen to The Specter, falling for his promises of being delivered to a world without pain and the mundane- burdensome responsibilities like taking care of someone else, paying bills or watching what was love sour over an undisclosed number of years.

She, with her curly black hair and pecan skin figured she could have had anyone she wanted while she waited night after night, some nights all night. That was what she told herself while she looked in the mirror, admiring the features of her lonesome face blinded by "prosperity." She used to pretend she and he were about to go out to dinner someplace special upon his return, or she would dress up in some sexy nightgown and await his arrival, mulling over what pose she was going to greet him with as he walked in through the door. *Incense or no incense?* Her face was all made up, her foundation and rouge, just right. Her hair had the perfect shine to it and it should have, with all the time she spent getting it together. The lipstick was the coup de grace, always the last detail.

"You look fantastic!" she told herself.

She looked in the mirror for a short while, then realized he was not coming. In one fell swoop, as became her custom with the usual epiphany, she washed her face almost immediately, throwing the lipstick and other makeup in the bathtub she never used anymore. The bathtub became full to the brim with the lipsticks, the foundations and the rouges she never got around to using from their previous lives, some with the price tags still attached to them. Her intentions were always good when she bought each and every one of them in those good old prosperous days.

Once The Specter took hold of her husband, she unknowingly became caught in a whirlwind leading her right to the reservation, by her husband's side. He was one of the lucky ones- he actually began realizing how The Specter was a master of lies. Once he felt himself losing his wife for good, standing in a doorway between life and death with The Specter urgently persuading him to come hither into darkness, Mr. Trotter looked behind him and actually felt a real possibility he would never see the life he had before ever again. Love actually saved him. And it was love that brought them to the church, where they decided they would start all over again. As a byproduct of love and a few grand, tender, greeting card moments, they decided The Specter, in the form of Mr. Trotter taking drugs, was no longer welcome in their lives- during those grand, tender, greeting card moments. *Ah, but a moment is but a moment.*

NINE

DEACON THOMAS BROUGHT the small meeting to order. "Gentlemen, Pastor Jenkins could not be here tonight, but is there any new news? Yes Deacon Curtis?"

"The choir complained about how the drum playing from that new young one is too loud, and something has to be done about it because they can barely hear themselves sing up there."

"Drums too loud....okay, who is in charge of the music ministry, Deacon Simms? Could you gather both parties and resolve that dispute please? Is there any more new news? No, then let us adjourn in a timely fashion- Deacon Carson please lead us out in prayer please."

"Dear heavenly father, we come just to say thank you, thank you for allowing us to fellowship in your house once again, and it is my prayer that we in the black community stop taking your grace for granted, Amen." The other deacons looked at him with a sneer. *What the heck kind of prayer was that?*

Home, again. *I would love to stay here, but I can't.* Then back to Church. Once Carson got home again, he knew he could go to bed early just to get back to Church early. Then to Church, then to another funeral, then back home. *My allegiance is to the dead and to a building.* What was to become of the reservation? There was so much death all around everyone, so much that no one could sustain. *Lord, we need you now.* How many had to perish?

Carson knew he needed rest, and there was a knock on his door. The hour was late and Carson desperately wanted his time to be his own. He wondered who it could be, again. When he opened the door, it was a young girl, dressed like a member of the choir, in a brown paper robe. Carson had never seen her before, ever.

"Deacon Carson, you're needed at the hospital!"

"Who *are* you? Ex-excuse me, I will be there," Carson replied. "Do you know who it is?"

"I only know that you are needed."

"Tell them I will be there." Carson turned to reach for his Bible. "Who are you and how do you know me?" he asked.

The girl was gone.

Upon entering the hospital, the same girl who stood in the doorway to Carson's flat appeared before the door of the patient he was to see.

"Who are you?" Carson asked again. She did not respond. Carson opened the door to find Pastor Jenkins bedridden, pale and shrinking before his eyes, with his wife beside him.

"Oh, Lord! Pastor! What happened?!"

"Deacon Carson, he cannot hear you," his wife replied. "He too became sick from the flood and kept it from everyone."

"What?! Are you telling me you have not told anyone about this?"

"No one."

"Why *me?*"

"Deacon Carson, my husband told me you are the only one he can really trust. He feels like you are his true friend. Deacon, he wants you to take over the duties of Pastor, in his place."

"WHAT?!- I- I don't know if I can, can do that! I mean, I can't do that! Wh- *are you serious?!*" Carson noticed that the girl who stood before the door was no longer there.

"He needs you right now, Deacon. Will you do it?"

"I- are you sure he wants *me?* I am no preacher!"

"Every man who has been called as a Deacon has a sermon in him and I am sure you can find more than one. Will you do it?"

"Y-yes. I, will give my best. I will do it but who will recognize me, what about the other Deacons?"

"It is already done."

Carson sat down beside the bed holding the hand of his friend dying of yellow fever- the same illness that took Ronnie. He sat, holding the hand of the old fool whom people said never knew any better than to cross plaids with stripes. Carson knew the people on the reservation never knew the man, always opting to be entertained instead of taught. *My Lord, Heavenly Father, there is so much to consider. Are you sure you want me in this position? What if I fail? I only now ask for your guidance. Decrease me, so that you may increase.*

Not another word came from Pastor's mouth, and Carson was not even sure Pastor heard him when he said they would always be friends. Before he slipped into unconsciousness for the last time, Carson asked him to say hello to his wife and son, and that he would make a great Pastor for the congregation waiting for him in the next world.

Dear Lord-

What do you really want with me, or do you want me at all? By the way, a lot of people here are not sure Jesus really even exists because they are only able to concentrate on their pain and nothing else. Now the question is, just what are they motivated to do? Then if he does exist, what would even the idea of Jesus want with me as a Pastor? Does he want me to shine a light for him? Be his Dea- uh- beacon of righteousness? Well, beacons of righteousness don't look like me according to the television channel broadcast from the city- medium skinned and wooly haired and beacons of righteousness don't act like me- walking into the city and challenging anybody on the street to a fight. The city wants to bring me up in its image, which could possibly mean dead. Every time I think of the picture of the white Jesus out by the guarded gate of the city symbolizing righteousness, I see myself as less than. When I look at myself in any mirror, I only see me. What do I do now?

The robe felt funny, and Carson wished the choir could go on singing forever. He sat in the makeshift pulpit and tried with all his might to ignore the broken, rotten egg yolks sliding down the glass in front of him unbelievers from the crowd continued throwing. *I am the one who needs protection now. Wait a minute, protection from what? These people do not scare me, they never did. If it is a fight they want, it is a fight I will give them. Then again, if the choir goes on singing, I will never have to get out of this chair.*

Dead silence. The choir stopped singing. Carson came out of his daydream long enough to realize it was finally time to preach. He got up, with Bible in hand and walked to the pulpit. He looked down at the Deacon row, which was empty. Upon news Carson would lead the church, the others resigned. All around the sanctuary, he saw blank stares, and some within the congregation were even asleep. In a back corner, within the negative faction of the congregation, stood The Specter, hooded, dark and menacing, his face hidden from view. It could be anyone Carson knew under the mars black robe for all he knew, but one thing was for certain; he was real. Some others chewed gum mindlessly and a few had eyes wide open, ready to hear every word.

"I don't know about you, but like the choir sang, I'm saved today!" Carson began.

Silence. "I said I don't know about you, but I'm saved today- isn't it good to be in the house of the Lord?!" Silence.

"What's the matter with you people today? Stand on your feet and give him some praise, come on, let's go!" A few people stood, while the rest in the congregation sat, bewildered, with heads tilted to either side.

"COME ON PEOPLE, LET'S GO, GIVE HIM SOME PRAISE!!!"

A few more rose to their feet, and then, an egg hit the glass off to the left.

"Hey look! Someone threw an egg- least I know you're awake!!" Wrong words. A shower of eggs hit the glass, to the point where Carson could no longer see the congregation. Welcome to the world, the Pulpit, the working week, the congregation and well, the church.

The clock read six as Carson had been sitting in Pastor Jenkins' small, private room for a long time since the service came to an abrupt end. Carson never wanted to leave that room again. Once he finally gathered the gumption to get up and go home, he only walked the roads, leaving his car behind. How did I even get myself into this? The right choice for Pastor? *Me*?!

Carson walked the dirt roads, seeing the drug users in their usual places, and many people going in and out of the casino. There were cars parked all around the casino; the gigantic cinder brick building that was the center of the reservation. The large number of cars indicated people from the city had come in to gamble. Carson walked over to the front door, still dressed in his robe. Over his head, a neon arrow pointed toward the door, as if a person intent on gambling needed any more nudging. Carson opened the door to find members of the congregation working and serving people from the city with much more zeal than they had ever shown within the church. Popping sounds and flashing colors of gold and silver coins fell into trays and plastic cups. Booze disappeared, bringing about false courage. Money won and lost, frustration, deals, propositions were made, with the people of the reservation selling each other short. The Specter stood within, there and everywhere, facing Carson and leaning forward, his posture revealing surprise that he entered into a house of sin. Carson accepted the fact he stood alone within a sea of denial as one turned to see him, then another, then another. People from the city looked upon Carson as if he was the most common trash.

"What are you doing here?" a man Carson saw once before said. He was dressed in a khaki and red uniform of the casino and his name tag read "MANAGER."

"I am only watching," Carson replied. I am getting a feel for my congregation and who they are."

"I don't want to offend or upset you, but could you get a feel for who they are in church, instead of here?" he asked. "You standing here is interfering with my business."

"Sir, I have not begun yet to interfere with your business, but trust me when I say- enjoy it while it lasts!"

"Sir, please leave, or I'll have someone put you out!" he said.

"Really?" Carson replied, surprised and standing erect. "Let's see you do that! Come on-tell one of your little goons to come over here and get some!"

"Sir, please leave- I don't want any trouble from you- please!" the manager pleaded with his hands forming a symbol of prayer. Prayer. *What are you doing servant?! Unclench your fists and rely on the power of prayer.*

Carson turned toward the door, and exited without a sound.

Out on the roads again and standing under a sky of ultramarine, Carson wished there was another way for the reservation to survive as far as income, but right then there was no other way. How did Pastor Jenkins feel about all this? Carson knew he wanted to do something about it, but what? *What can I do about it? Just sit back and pray for them to go away? The power of prayer.*

Carson continued walking by groups of people through the summer heat of the night as beads of sweat begin rolling from his forehead. He spotted one or two from the congregation earlier, the blank faces, the gum chewers. They stopped to look at Carson- the flop- and he wondered would they ever come back to The Church once everybody understood the reality that Pastor Jenkins was not coming back. No one even said hello, they only stared and when Carson passed, they snickered. *Let them laugh. I'll give them something to laugh at.* Carson passed by a fat lady giving physical fitness advice to someone who actually listened. He passed by another lady wearing heavy makeup reading palms at a table for fifty cents beside a round, dim ball of light sitting atop a table draped in a shining green tablecloth.

"Would you like your palm read sir? I can tell you your future!"

"No ma'am, no thank you," Carson replied. "I know what it is already."

A man rushed past Carson and almost knocked him down. Kids ran by him in the night, playing with toy pistols. Off in the distance, he saw Leslie, his dirty blonde wig almost covering his face that most of the time he actually preferred to keep hidden. Though the heat was considerable, Leslie held himself, clutching his worn blazer and crossing his bare legs as if in the dead of winter.

A group of kids walked by, all of whom wore their hair in dreadlocks and all of whom were shirtless with their pants hanging down past their buttocks, exposing their underwear. In the short time they took to pass, nearly every word Carson heard from their mouths was profane. The whole lot of them were a bad jingle, a rogue playbill suggesting a deadly attitude of the young black male still existed toward his own self, even after so many years of hardship, choosing to ignore so many of life's lessons. Their hostile, unaesthetic outlooks rendered them as nuisances lacking the good sense to realize how it was their own minds telling them how everyone around *wished* they would just die.

The choir stopped singing, again. And to Carson's surprise, the congregation seemed more full than it was the week before. *Maybe they came to see the young guy fall on his face again. Maybe, just maybe, they think they have found a new stooge to entertain them.*

Carson rose from his chair, and strode to the pulpit, without a Bible. Blank stares. Heads tilted to either side. Some waiting just to get back out again. *Today will be my lucky day at the casino. Seven, eleven, HA!!* Carson pulled out a piece of chewing gum, and put it in his mouth and began chewing. The blank faces turned stunned- they were awake after all.

"Who am I y'all?!" Carson asked, walking around the pulpit, waving his arms in nonchalance. "Come on, who am I? Can't guess? Don't know? I'M YOU, that's who I am!! I don't know nothin', and I don't even know I don't know nothin'! Don't care 'bout nothin' or nobody, not even myself! Why do you all come here? Tell me that?! What are you looking for out of your lives? The way you all live around here, I CAN SWEAR YOU DON'T EVEN BELIEVE IN GOD!! You let drug dealers give drugs to your own kids, and half of you are taking them yourselves! You are obviously not grateful for anything you have. Do you know what your problem is? Let me guess-you're sad you're not living in the city, or perhaps even that you're not white, for those of you who have been watching too much television. Your egos are written all over your faces, but so is your low self-esteem. What's it going to be? Jesus, or continuing to wait on the lottery? When you decide, let me know!"

Carson left right out the front door of the church for a walk, leaving the congregation behind. Later, he sat in Pastor Jenkins' study, asking The Lord for guidance. He opened his eyes, finally to the sparse room and looked down at the desk where he sat. Carson had not once even opened the drawers of the desk, assuming them to be empty. He opened a drawer to find a small envelope marked "Deacon Carson," and opened it. It was a letter from Pastor Jenkins.

Dear Deacon Carson;

Once I knew I was sick, I made the choice for you to lead this congregation. I have watched you for some time my friend. I saw when your beloved Alexis passed when she gave birth to Ronnie and though you were shaken, you never lost faith in The Lord. I watched you when Ronnie passed on. While lesser men would have given up, you stayed firm. You have what it takes to lead the congregation. You are well aware of the evil forces outside the church, but are you aware of the forces within it? This task will be difficult, that is why The Lord has chosen you. Do not ever doubt yourself again.

Always Your Pastor
Carl

Albumen clouds mixed with black ink gathered overhead outside, threatening rain, yet Carson felt empowered. People meandered on the streets, here, there. Carson saw the neglected buildings and their watermarks from the flood, the very stigma of exposure all over the reservation. He felt lonesome, missing his son and wondering will he ever meet anyone on earth like Alexis ever again.

TEN

DEAR LORD, THESE are my letters I wrote to you. My only wish is for them to be heard:

Am I truly single?

What must I do
To make you love me?
What is necessary
To show you how I care?

I ask you, The Lord above me
To keep and hold me before
I choose to explore-
Out there

Do I dare reveal I care
To go out there to bear
The misery and suffering of
Someone who may not have
You Lord?

What if I look within at my sin
Amid your chagrin- again,
That I am guilty of
Maybe I should come correct before I
Go looking for love

Looking for love
in a lot of seedy minds and places
Since she has been gone
A boatload of pain and a lot of empty faces
Later- to sway her- doggone
I gotta stand right, look right
Brush and keep my head tight
While I wait for her- uh- you O Lord

Again I ask that you above
Keep and hold me before
I look for love

Am I the fool on the hill
Loaded on the word and pills to the gills
Genuinely pretending I'm filled
and one disrespectful
act away from a kill
Because truly, my rage has
Come of age, and take a step
Back, even in broad daylight
Because I'm out of my cage
To wage another page of war against
Days upon days of having no one
And nothing to share or care
For life- with?

Well I'll go on then, and mix in
With the rest, telling myself
I'm blessed through test after
Test, and eventually, I become my own
Biggest pest, stressed, at my behest, dressed
In my Sunday best

No time left for you-
On my way to better things honey, but
Maybe it's not a smart thing
To cling or to sing praises
For those who are just men
or to wing
This thing called self-esteem
Yet, it might be better to look
Within at my sin, again, I that have
committed
Fallen short- convicted
People pleaser- addicted
Jesus Christ- restricted
On self will- afflicted
What am I driving?
Afflicted
I'll kill you man!
Afflicted

But Father, in the end
Looking within at my sin
Yet again, despite your
Chagrin, I still win and I'll
Keep coming in to
Your house, as long as you'll have me

To my wife, the wife of a Pastor:

I remember you, as each rain
Drop touches the ground
As each leaf falls from the dying trees
There is no day that passes where
I cannot see your face in my mind

I remember now times
Between me and you
The nights I passed you like a ship
And never saw the truth
I smiled for strangers
And forgot when it came to you
To say I love you, now you're
Gone and the simple truth-is-
I am alone and I miss
The bliss, when I closed
My eyes for your kiss- kiss
And I wish- wish for your
Touch- touch, tears- fears
Wash over me when I open
My eyes to the years- years
See how they ran away from
You and me- day by day
O Dear Lord, her sweet love
That thing I prayed- for
Give me the chance to pass
Through that imaginary door
To tell her how I was such a fool
To pass by each night like a ship

On a trip that had me stand
Holding hands with complete strangers
Gasping for breath until their
Deaths, and who will go down
In the grave with me?

I will always remember you
As rain still falls to the ground
As snow falls upon the dead leaves
Underneath the bare trees
There is no day that passes
When I cannot see your face
In my mind

For my own sanity;

Dear Lord-
Have you ever had a helper?
Someone, to help you,
Answer all the prayers?

Let me say I'd like to help you,
Me, as one, with barely a direction

Dear Lord-
Have you ever needed comfort?
In the midst, of all the things
that people
Take you through

Let me say I'd like to help you
With a spot of tea or a blanket
I'll drop what I'm doing

What a chore it is to step outside myself
To see the world rushing by
Leaving people in its wake
The battle is yours but it seems so heavy-
Against eyes and hearts of us who
Feel hot and cold

Let me say I'd like to help you
A soldier, a bodyguard
Against the arrows and the slings
I just want you to know that I'm here

Broken glass lied all over the ground in the alleyway. Smoke came from his nose as well as his mouth. Kids no more than twelve stood around watching him in amazement. Ace was just another drug dealer who happened to partake of his product, in that case, marijuana. He made no attempt to conceal his doings, in fact he *wanted* someone to come up to him to ask him why he was doing what he was doing. There were not many people on the roads on that Saturday morning, but that smoking episode was Ace's way of trying to get attention.

"Excuse me," Carson said, amid the smoke in his face. None of them saw Carson as he came up to them, but at the sound of his voice, the other kids took off running. Not Ace. He just continued smoking.

"Excuse me," Carson said again.

He stopped to look at Carson, knowing full well he heard him the first time.

"Whut?!" he asked indignantly. Anyone who might dare interrupt his being a complete fool deserved the look, the look of "who the hell are you?"

"Do you know God?" Carson asked.

He coughed, as if to keep himself from laughing. "Do I know God? Nawle, do he know me?"

"Yes, he does, and he does not like what you are doing."

"I paid for this, so I'm gon' smoke it!"

"You stupid fool!" Ace looked at Carson in shock. "I'm not talking about what you paid or didn't pay for, I'm talking about why are you standing out here so miserable, trying to take other little kids down with you! See here, dum dum, if you wanna smoke crap, that's your choice, do it alone. If I see you out here again with little kids I will beat you up and down this street in front of everyone! YOU UNDERSTAND ME!"

"I'm gon' tell my father!"

"Go ahead, punk, tell who you want! I'm the Pastor on this reservation now- you tell him I'll be at the church if he wants to see me. I'll be watching you!" Carson took the marijuana from his hand and smashed it on the ground. As he walked away, Ace only stood still, pouting.

ELEVEN

THE CHOIR TOOK a seat, and again, Carson strode to the pulpit. Looking out into the crowd beyond the glass, he tried to make eye contact with everyone before he began. Everyone.

"As you look at Corinthians, chapter eight, verse two, I want to address you from the subject "The Grace of God…..The Grace… of God.

No doubt, many of you have lost quite a bit, perhaps everything, and perhaps, like me, even a loved one or even two, like me. Some of you, like me, may even be questioning God right now, asking 'Why me o Lord, why me?' How is it that you can allow those who openly do not believe in you, based on the way they live, to prosper? Indeed, when I think of my own son, and what a good boy he was, it makes me angry now that he's gone." Carson felt eyebrows raise throughout the crowd.

"I'm just being real people- I'm angry! He believed in God because his daddy did, and that's all right! 'Use me as a crutch until you can stand on your own,' I always told him. At least he was willing to believe in you Lord, against this backdrop of so many who choose to use drugs, who choose to sell drugs and who choose to drink and smoke their lives away here as if you do not exist, I have to ask 'Why?'

Verse two says 'During a great trial of affliction...there was abundant joy.' Abundant joy? Lord in our pain we ask, how can you let fools who openly do not believe in you dodge financial crisis or, or hunger, uh, maybe the grass looks a little greener on the other side, from our side, on this reservation, this hole of a place, the depths of the earth! Well my brothers and my sisters maybe it seems that way because we make it so, maybe it's our attitude that needs adjusting, right smack in the middle of this affliction called the flood, where we have lost so many, where it doesn't look like life is even worth living for some of us- it seems the sun never shines here, where we are, it seems someone is always losing a job, losing a home, losing a loved one, losing courage, losing heart, and even losing faith but I tell you we do have a reason to keep on believing, and it has nothing to do with whether you live on the reservation, or the city, or where you work!"

There was movement within the crowd, and Carson sensed an excitement in the church even he had never felt before.

"It has to do with the fact that we too should have been dead, but God saw fit to show mercy! God saw fit to show his grace! Those loved ones we have lost, those people who prayed for us over and over again, would be disappointed if we stopped living and drank our lives away, smoked our lives away, gambled our lives away! I'm tellin' you now, I DON'T WANT NONE OF IT!!

I get tired of waiting for The Lord sometimes, like you do, wondering when He's gonna make right what ain't right- but if he did, would YOU be here when he was done?!" All over the sanctuary, people began to stand. Many even began approaching the glass.

"I'll wait on him, and be of good courage! I'll keep on waiting- though I'm hurting inside! I'll keep on waiting- though outsiders all around me try to make be believe that I am less than!" The congregation began to pound on the glass in excitement. "I'll keep on waiting- though others try to make me think that because I am black I am incapable of thought, of intellect, and I just can't get past hating myself!

Lord, you are in control of all things! All things!! My pain won't last forever! I won't live in church forever- I'll go out into the world and praise your name! I won't feel like I'm less than forever- soon I'll stand face to face with the truth and understand it's all sleight of hand and makeup coming together to make my oppressors appear more powerful than they actually are! I won't be poor, forever- when I'm with you, I won't need money, and I won't even need a ride! I won't be homeless forever- you are preparing a place for me and my brothers, black and white or wherever they come from- a place where color won't matter- money won't matter- jobs won't matter and where I live won't matter! Size won't matter, speed won't matter, what you drive won't matter, how much you drink and smoke won't matter, what church you go to won't matter, and what you think of me won't matter, only what you believe!!

Only what you believe! Only what you believe! Only what you believe!! So believe in Him!!! Believe in God's grace!!" Believe in His love!!

TWELVE

NIGHT AFTER NIGHT and day after day, Leslie sat on the bench, smack in the middle of the reservation. He gave off an ungodly odor from drinking, smoking and never taking good care of himself. People who had their own problems walked by him pointing, some even laughing at the very idea of an old, stinky man sitting in front of everyone dressed like a woman, his dirty blonde wig falling off his head. Sometimes it looked as if he was asleep, and then it looked as if he just had his head down. Leslie was a diversion, a wonderful novelty for the entire reservation. No one's problems were that bad if they came outside and saw Leslie sitting on the same dirty bench in front of everyone with his mini skirt and his crossed, skinny legs the color of coal, always unshaven, bearing stubby, white hair.

"Is that a man or a woman?" people asked themselves, until it started becoming clear by his unshaven face becoming more grizzly by the day.

"Ah, it's a man who *thinks* he's a woman," people replied to the question when it became absolutely clear.

During the day, no one ever went near Leslie. The people on the reservation who requested Leslie's services wanted them in complete darkness, and chances were they were some of the people who walked by laughing during the daylight hours. Those "friends" of his fought to make sure no one ever knew who they were, making sure the darkness they transgressed in was always *complete.* No one there ever knew how Leslie was once a promising young law student at a small university in the city, long before the reservation itself and long before the flood. Always lonesome, he struggled to keep an image of dignity, and there were many times he actually had to remember how his once proud family had migrated from Nigeria to The United States years before. The Specter toyed with Leslie in a different way; where most turned to drugs when they believed there was no hope, Leslie buried himself in his low self esteem. Leslie had suffered much mental and physical abuse when he was a young boy, particularly on those days when his father would come home fresh from fighting for his dignity in the white world, blaming him for all his troubles, giving him the verbal and physical end of a belt, a hot iron or anything else to cause him pain. When his father lost his job because of drinking, days came when he peddled his effeminate son as a whore on the streets so they could eat. The Specter had Leslie believe his abuse was the way life was supposed to be, that it was normal. Leslie had one thing in common with other slaves of The Specter however; not wanting anything to do with people, though Leslie needed people to carry out his feeling of "normal."

On a day under an ironic feel of bright, hopeful sunshine with people who still had their own problems walking by and laughing, it looked as if Leslie might be asleep. He wasn't asleep at all. He had been delivered by The Specter to a place far away from the reservation, a place no less pleasant than the bench, but a place nonetheless away from the curious, laughing onlookers who would always have their own problems to live with.

THIRTEEN

MIKE CHAMBERS, NOT to be redundant, was a bully and a jerk, and Vince wondered why he never came for revenge of any kind for what happened that past day in practice, not in the hallways, and not on the field. According to Coach Turk, he was the star on the team. *Maybe he doesn't have time to worry about somebody like me, a junior who won't even get much playing time for at least another year.*

Life at Redemption High was not total hell for Vince, in fact he rather enjoyed it. Vince was a decent student, except in geometry, and once he began dating Olivia, everything- the practices, the sweating, the yelling and the expectations from his father became more bearable. Any day at school was okay, as long as she was there. The first time Vince walked Olivia to one of her classes, she put her arm under his before they left her locker as everything and everybody in the halls became an insignificant blur for them both. Other students huddled, stared into space and schemed amongst themselves here and there, but Vince and Olivia never saw them. In fact, once Vince fell in love with Olivia, part of him just assumed everybody else was in love or looking for love as well. They had to be, because it felt too good.

The two of them had lunch together every day, and though he had not said it, Olivia knew Vince had fallen for her. They sat, shoulder to shoulder everyday with their backs to the loud mass of students running back and forth through the cafeteria.

"Frankie, eventually, you will have to get saved," Olivia said, taking Vince's hand.

"Saved? From what?"

"Saved from *sin*," Olivia replied.

"Saved from sin, how do I do that?" Vince asked. "Does that mean I have to go to church all the time?"

"It will probably mean you'll have to go more than you do now, but Vince, I am saved, and you're not. We are of two different yokes. If we are going to be together, we have to be of the same yoke."

"What do you mean, the same *yoke*?"

"I mean that since I am saved from sin, I am on another level in my life with God. Let me explain- there will come a time when the world will come to an end. When it does, God will save only those who have declared his son Jesus Christ as Lord and Savior."

"Who exactly is Jesus Christ?" Vince asked.

"The Son of God."

"So I have to declare him as my Lord and…"

"*Savior,*" Olivia whispered in his ear.

"How do I do that?"

"Come to the church with me next week and see for yourself. We have a new preacher and it was a little rough going at first. I think he's gonna be okay though. When he is ready to receive new members, come down to the front and give your life to Jesus."

"Come to church with you?" Vince asked.

"Yeah, I mean Vince, if you love me, we are going to have to be of the same yoke. Please Vince, come, I mean, there's this guy Eric who likes me a lot, he's always showing up at my locker, asking me out, and he's even come over to our house and met my mother! He likes me, but I like you Vince! Please, come to church with me!" Olivia pleaded.

"This guy, Eric, or whoever he is, came over to your house you say?"

"Yeah."

"And he met your mother?"

"Yeah."

"Does your mother like him?"

"She likes the fact that he's saved!"

"He's *saved*, huh?"

"Yeah, and he wasn't when I met him here at school, I think he did it just for me."

"Oh, really?" Vince asked, becoming irritated.

"Yes, really, and Vince if you get saved, and be my boyfriend, that means he will leave me alone!"

Vince looked down at the table in front of him and winced, nearly closing his eyes. "Am I your boyfriend, Olivia, even though I am not saved?"

"Yeah, Vince, you're my boyfriend."

"How did you know that I love you?"

"I can see it in your eyes when you look at me. I saw it the first time you came to my locker. If I mean anything to you, I need you to come to the church."

FOURTEEN

The following Sunday morning, Olivia showed up at Vince's house in a big, old rusted black Cadillac that left behind a thick trail of black smoke slow to dissipate into the air.

"Vince, who that outside?" David asked.

"Dad, that's my girlfriend, and we're goin' ta' church!"

Vince's father stood, looking through the dirty windows of their modest dwelling to see a beautiful, fair skinned young lady in a simple, knee length, dark colored dress. Her legs were bare and she wore black tennis shoes, sifting her way through the old trash cans and other relics laying in the dirt before his door. In seeing her, David was reminded when pretty girls were available at around five cents a dozen during his playing days- for the good players though, those who were going on to make money in places like the city and other pastures of green. When he had potential, they gave him a passing glance, was all.

To David, pretty girls were a status symbol; there was one in particular he remembered- Tamara- he did not know her last name- whom he fell in love with. She was pretty, like Olivia- fair skin, long hair. He could not remember if she was a church girl though. He kinda doubted it.

"Tamara, my name David- and- I, I on the football team!" he said proudly.

She held a pencil to her mouth in a coy manner, knowing she had complete control of the situation. "I know who you is. What 'chu want?"

"Will you go with me? W-you be my gal?"

"*Maybe*. I'll see 'bout it."

As soon as it was evident he was not going to be one of those breadwinners, a glance from Tamara became something rare.

"Hey Tamara!" David called out.

"Who is *you?*" she snapped.

Any chance he had with Tamara disappeared with the drugs he used, but David believed The Specter was never too far away in his life. Standing and peering through his filthy window, David knew he had wasted a chance in life and his son's girlfriend- his pretty girlfriend- was only a reminder of that. There was something about this girl, though. He would have traded them all- those uppity, pasty-faced Tamaras who would have never remembered him separated from a buck the next day, for a girl like Olivia. Vince opened the door in front of him, and the closer she got, the more beautiful she became.

Vince put his arms around her and kissed her on the cheek, bringing his father back to the cold, harsh present. "Dad, this is my girlfriend Olivia."

"Pleased to meet you, sir," Olivia said, outstretching her hand.

"No, no, the pleasure is all mine," David replied in an effort to speak proper with a dry taste of envy. "Where now, are y-takin' my son?"

"Church," Olivia replied, politely, suspecting he already knew where she and Vince were heading.

"I hear the pastor who took over is no good-people say he can't preach at all and they is lookin' for somebody else already," David said looking directly into Olivia's eyes, to see if he could get a rise from her.

"It's obvious you were not there last week!" Olivia shot back. "Vince we're gonna be late- nice to meet you sir!" she said, walking away with a nonchalant wave of her hand.

"Later dad!" Vince yelled, running behind Olivia to catch up.

"Yeah, later," David mumbled. Olivia had not even budged and did not bother waving goodbye, making David feel as old as he really was.

Once the two of them got to the car, a big, fat white haired black man got out from the front seat, came around the car and opened the back passenger door. The man even wore a dusty old black chauffeur hat.

"Vince, this is my Uncle Bobby, Uncle Bobby, meet my *boyfriend* Vince!"

"Hello," Vince said, looking up at her Uncle in astonishment. "Thank you very much!"

"Don't mention it young man. I've heard so much about you. If *Olivia* likes you, then you must be okay!"

Vince got into the back seat of the car and sat beside Olivia. Looking into his eyes, she took his hand.

"Where to kids?" her Uncle called.

Olivia laughed. "Church Bobby, please."

Riding along, Vince put his arms around Olivia and held her close. He ran his hand through her hair, and Olivia gave him a look of love he would never forget. Bobby was such a nice man to drive, and the two of them never even got an impression he was peeking through the rear view mirror.

"Will your mother be at church tonight?" Vince asked, when he was finally able to take a breath after seeing the look in Olivia's eyes from point blank range.

"No, she has to work today at the casino," she whispered. "Uncle Bobby gonna take us, and bring us back." Olivia's eyes welled and a single tear found its way down her cheek. Vince did not ask her what was the matter, he figured she was happy. She rested her head upon his chest and did not say another word during the drive.

The car bellowed and hissed its way down the dirt road in a cloud of smoke, arriving a little less than a half mile to The Baptist church of The Reservation. The graffiti covered cinder block building did not a have a marquee; its purpose shifted through a late summer wind outside in red letters on a banner tied to metal poles with loose foundations in the dirt.

There were few cars outside, but then, there were few cars on the reservation. Most of the people who came on Sundays walked, since the church was in the center of everything.

"Here we are kids," Bobby said, "The Baptist Church! Have a good service!"

Olivia gently pulled through the door and Vince noticed how the temperature inside the building changed slightly to be even warmer and he held Olivia's hand even tighter. The texture of the dirt beneath his feet outside followed him inside because there was no floor. There were many rusted folding chairs forming uneven rows. Vince saw a makeshift wooden cross at the front decorated with plastic flowers behind a wall of glass. Off to the side of it, sat a few instruments-guitars, an old paint-peeled piano and a drum set, waiting for their musicians. There were a good number of people there that Sunday, with an atmosphere of laughter and jest- the opposite of what Vince had anticipated. There were kids running, and people slapping hands in the air. People had feet over the backs of chairs and the rows became even more crooked as time progressed and more people came. Once the two of them sat down, Vince heard talk from people around him of later meeting at the casino and how many of them had come to see the foolish new pastor fall on his face again.

"They need ta' get somebody else in here 'cause this guy aint' no good!" one man said. "I know he took over in a bad situation, but they need ta' better screen these people before they let em' up there!"

"He did real good last week, but eventually, he gon' git ate alive, no doubt!" said another.

"Why do they say these things about your pastor?" Vince asked.

"A couple weeks ago when he preached, he made people really mad," Olivia explained. "He took over for our other pastor, Pastor Jenkins, who died. I really think today, he's gonna show everybody the real word- again!"

Why is everything behind glass? Is he afraid of someone?" Vince asked.

"People here can get really mean," Olivia replied. "They throw things."

"Oh, okay!" Vince replied, feeling unsure for a moment as to why he was there. "Are you going to sit beside me? Please stay with me."

"I can't," Olivia whispered. "Sit right here, I'll be back."

"Where are you…" Olivia walked off to a side door, appeared up on the stage and sat at the drum set. She was then joined by a woman at the piano and two other men took up the guitars. Once they began playing, Olivia looked at Vince from the stage and winked. A drummer?

As Olivia and the rest of the band played, a tall, white blond man came out from behind a curtain and sat in a chair among a few other black men on the stage, off to the side of the musicians. The man leaned over on one hand, and Vince noticed a disappointed look on his face as he surveyed the surly crowd. Once the musicians finished playing, He got up, and began ranting and raving about Jesus and what he called "running to Egypt," displaying crazy hand gestures. He moaned about how "people out there" were working their jobs and choosing to spend their money on any and everything but insuring the spreading of the news of Jesus Christ.

"There you go…runnin' to Egypt and aspiring to live like so many people do in the city!" the man said, which was where Vince imagined he was from. "You got no time for Jesus, but you got time for your casino and your smoking and your booze and anything else taking your mind away from the great one.. the one who has all power. You're not giving him what he deserves.. and he knows it." As suddenly as the man rose, he sat back down again, which was the queue for the musicians to continue on.

When the man talked, Vince felt funny, guilty even. What were people supposed to do with their money?

My name is Frank Carson, and my only goal in life was to help people, that is, after I got sober and acquired an ability to think about anyone else but myself. I was one of those types who walked around lamenting over how I was so misunderstood, with a bottle of booze in one hand and a small radio tuned in to an easy listening station I knew I would never have a conflict with in my other. There were many days and nights when it took more than just looking into a mirror to get to the truth about me. I did not like who I was. In the day to day hustle and the running back and forth between people, I upheld the right to be a heathen and forgot why I was even alive, which was my problem to begin with. I'm okay with me now, but I sometimes still have my doubts, coming from a black world where I think I have to prove myself all the time, yet I imagine my behavior is beyond reproach. What world is that? The world you and I live in- the real world, the working world. I mean it, I always had this deep down desire to help other people, so I joined a church and in time, became a Deacon. The last thing I thought I would ever do was become a Pastor. I have my doubts right now and I cannot think of a worse time to find that out with our numbers so sparse as a result of a lack of faith. I remember the letter Pastor Jenkins left behind for me and maybe it is not doubt I feel, but fear. Nevertheless, I ask for your help as I go out here today, against the naysayers. I will forge ahead. Let there be one here today who might hear the words you have put in my mouth.

Once the musicians brought their song to an end, Vince noticed the pastor everyone was talking about walk out to the stage through a side door. He was dressed in a black graduation robe with a white cross painted upon his chest. Instead of sitting in a chair in the middle of the pulpit that was obviously meant for him, he walked right to the makeshift podium. The crowd was without a sound- the entertainment for the day had arrived.

"Ladies and gentlemen, I greet you on this Sunday morning with a sense of purpose; a purpose that will open your eyes to see how as long as we are in this building, we are not outside in the world evangelizing- a purpose that will allow you to see we actually have enough members- but rather, it is *disciples* we need. This purpose will open your heart and allow you to let yourselves be used by The Lord, and last but not least a purpose that will always keep you alert to the presence of Satan himself, and to be ready to witness, despite the fact he works so hard to keep you in darkness.

I turn your attention now to Psalm 141, verses four through six and it reads as follows;

"Incline not my heart to practice any evil thing, to practice wicked works with men that work iniquity: and let me not eat of their dainties. Let the righteous smite me; it shall be a kindness: and let him reprove me; it shall be an excellent oil, which shall not break my head: for yet my prayer also shall be in their calamities. When their judges are overthrown in stony places, they shall hear my words; for they are sweet."

I come here today to ask you a simple question, if you will indulge me, giving me a few moments of your time; What if hell is here on earth? What if hell....is here on earth? Almost from the time we were able to speak as children, we all in this place have had a concept of heaven- that place with the puffy clouds and dirt free white robes. People sitting over here and yonder there in our imagination, playing harps and perhaps even preparing banquet tables with gracious spreads of food adorned with white roses. More importantly though, it is a place to meet Jesus, the very thing those of us who believe in God have been waiting for all our lives. When it comes to heaven, everything in our mind's eye is either draped, grown or painted white. Snow falls, but it is not cold- rain may fall, but it is not wet. When rain falls in heaven we instead get all the wonderful, glistening, splendid effects without any of the possible side effects like floods, bloating, house damage and etc.

Forget heaven for a moment- let's talk about hell. What if you found out through some grand conspiracy of how drugs and alcohol were really objects to be used, to be passed out, to keep you down, keep you miserable keep you unknowing? What if you found out that jealousy, envy- a want for others to fail and fall flat on their faces, was one of the things which actually forms this very idea of hell itself? We have our visions of hell, as well as heaven. You, standing in a place that is on fire, with some guy in a red suit, with horns, who is seeing to it you feel numbing pain for all the nasty things you have ever done. You- standing in a place tied to a chair where every lie you have ever told is played back to you and you are not allowed to say a word in your defense. You- strapped to a rack with your arms and legs outstretched-watching a video of all the times you ever stole something and no one knew about it but you. You then proceeded to ignore the guilt by burying it deep within yourself until the day came where you just felt nothing anymore. You- enjoying the sight of so much killing for entertainment that human lives just don't mean anything anymore. You- walking by and not caring for any child who might need you. Hell is not a complicated *place,* or *person,* or *thing,* it just involves your pain and your guilt and your greed and all your other vices-that's all. Some people might say our very vision of hell is manufactured by things in the media, perhaps by your favorite channel- the one channel broadcast from the city. If that is true, is not our vision of heaven subject to the same scrutiny?

What if each and every one of us has created our own personal hell? What if the idea of hell itself for me turned out to be an inability to put God before anything else in my life? Any consequences which may come with that, I would have to live with them, here on earth, right? You all are sitting there looking at me like you don't know what I'm talking about, but I promise you by the time I'm finished, you will! Somebody come on with an Amen here, help me out!"

The crowd sat silent, some even stunned. Vince looked at Olivia, who winked at him again, and nodded.

"What if I learned something that could prove to be valuable to the entire world and no one knew about it but me? Let's say I had a choice; If I shared the thing, the world would prosper. If I kept it to myself, I would become financially rich beyond my wildest dreams. What would I do? Well, what would you do? If I chose to be selfish, keep the thing to myself, would that form a version of hell, right here on earth?

So I chose, hypothetically and solely in the interest of money and greed, to keep this thing to myself. I simply do not want the world to have it. I mean, if the world had it, where would that put me? If I had the thing, or we'll call it the knowledge, to myself, I could choose to help someone else whenever I felt like it, and look like a hero, instead of giving thanks to The Lord. Sure, I like helping others, but what good is helping someone else if I can't tell anyone about it?"

Some in the crowd snickered, while others sat, uneasy and frowning.

"Do all these things I have just mentioned form a hell, perhaps for you, right here on earth? Can the money you ever win from the casino soothe your concerns and worries if indeed you ever choose to rely solely on yourself? I know many of us have financial problems right now and in fact, financial problems and living on the reservation go hand in hand- don't they? Yeah, but living on the reservation and low self esteem does not necessarily go hand in hand! Living on the reservation and not believing in The Lord, they don't have to go hand in hand! Nobody said when we found The Lord that trouble here on earth would never come to our door! But I'm here to tell you trouble won't last always- when you believe in Jesus! Dark clouds and rain won't last always, when you believe in Jesus! You can call on him anytime- in the morning, or even the midnight hour!"

Many in the congregation stood on their feet and applauded, including Vince.

"Hell, here on earth. What about relationships? Imagine, for a moment, that I'm married. What if I went behind my wife's back, every chance I got? Are those actions not hell in themselves?

What if, relying on myself, I chose to subscribe to all the latest trends including new kinds of sexy clothing, new flavors of alcohol, only to end up right in the same smelly dark place I was in before? They don't advertise about that! Try this, taste that, and it'll put you back in the same hole you were in- how can I sell a deep, dark hole? How can I sell depression and despair? How can I sell no way out? How can I sell anger and frustration? Don't make no sense, do it?! Guess what?! Somebody is sellin' all that stuff to YOU in different flavors and colors!! I can sell a better way of life, though you might not have a dime- I can sell a brighter day- even if there are clouds all over the sky- I can tell you about somebody who can give you joy, even though people may let you down, even though YOU might let someone down- JESUS!! JESUS!! These destructive ways of life… they make you feel good! I mean, isn't that what life is all about, feeling good? What then, if I walk outside on this reservation, and see my neighbor might have a little bit more than I have? Will I still feel good then? What if I became someone who was unable to forgive another when they made a mistake? Is that a form of hell?

What if, every time I came to church and yelled 'I've got the victory!' and that phrase meant someone else had to lose? Does God not stand for everyone? You and I, sitting here now, have to believe, no matter what may come, that he does!"

No eggs hit the windows, and the negative faction who usually took their place in the corner had walked out. They took The Specter with them. All around the small sanctuary, people stood and applauded. Olivia waved her hands from behind the drum set. Pastor Carson came out through the side door, from behind the protective glass with no fear. He stood in the middle of the crowd, directly in front of Vince.

"You came through boy! Good job!" one in the crowd yelled.

"I was put in this place I suppose, for a reason, besides a lack of money," Carson said, to which the crowd laughed.

"I am a witness to adults who have defiled themselves and who have mated over the years with curse after curse through generations until there are now no distinguishing features among our young, save curiosity. In summer, it rains here often, and whenever it does the sound of the raindrops remind me of how this place is so small. I see the faces of no one here underneath the clouds- they are all the same to me- the same mentality- the same shattered dreams. Whenever I lay down to sleep, that's all I ever see anymore. We can change that, you and me- right here! Right now!"

September, 2050- Pastor's diary

Today was like any other here on the reservation; a late summer day sprinkled with a hint of autumn. The remaining trees are still somewhat green, but there is a touch of red throughout the leaves. Monday morning, and I drove to the city to evangelize. There was not too much traffic on the dirt roads and I felt like I was the only one outside- like a road leading outside the reservation had opened up for me. Under a red-orange sun, I witnessed a tear in the vastness of space. It was like a ripped piece of paper through reality, and the closer I got to it, the larger it became. I drove right through it to what appeared to be another world. I believed I was still on the reservation, but it all felt different, like I was another person all together- a person who made a difference. I was not even sure of what I had done, but I knew I had done something to help someone else. The shanties making up the reservation before the tear became two and three story houses with front yards, driveways, and cars parked out front once I passed through the rift . There was no gate and no guards with guns. There was no trash strewn over the grounds, only clean white dotted lines that delineated newly paved roads. The skies were cereulean blue and full of hope, and I knew in the distance an opportunity of some sort awaited me. Moreover, I had a vision of the person I wanted to be; someone who remained surprised and appalled at signs of injustice. I drove down a brand new road when I saw a man who I usually always saw on the shoulder- one of the black nomads- filthy, with all his belongings in a shopping cart and either thumbing a ride or begging for money. Once I saw him beyond the tear, he was doing none of those things. He stood still and erect, clean shaven and wearing a suit. At the moment I came through, he walked away from his cart of belongings as if to say he did not need them anymore. He actually shed a part of himself- tore himself away from material things weighing him down. He looked right at me as I passed, carrying a sign with him which read "I did it- you can do it too!"

FIFTEEN

THIS IS DAVID, callin' ta' you! I ain't got nowhere else ta' go. Who else gon' listen ta' me now? I hate livin' 'round here. I'm thinkin' what it be like to have enough money to lift me above this place an' these ol' raggly people. I wonder what it be like, right, ta' have so much money, it won't matter one bit to nobody whether I was black or white. Listen ta' me- I want so much money, the cash and cars I would buy with it would make things right wit' everybody. I done let so many people down. If I got money an' people make 'dem nasty faces at me when I drive down th' road, I cin just go on home to a big white mansion far 'way from 'dem- and swim in some money. Maybe, if you gimme money, a young, pretty ol' gal like the one who came here for my boy will stop an' look at me an' won't think I am too old! The only reason- the ONLY reason- I would ever come back here when I git rich is to show 'em how good I'm doin'. I can be like Old Jed Clampett long ago inside the television, go from a nobody to a somebody overnight. The dif'rence, though, between me and him is he a nice guy, and I ain't like that. I really don't want a thing to do with people, except to push 'em outta my way. Money make everything okay, seeing how so many people fightin' over it. It would make me okay with me when I look at myself in th' mirror, you know, I can say HA without really sayin' it loud is what I'm livin' fo'. I'll move outta this place, and take my son with me, but if he don't wanna go, then ta' hell with him too, you know what 'um sayin'? I'll live somewhere where I ain't got ta see nobody's face no mo', be they black or white. I can't stand lyin', cheatin', an' connivin' people who just out for a buck. That was one thing you taught me- how ta' spot 'em.

In Carson's mind, driving down the road toward the city, Ronnie had already fallen asleep in the passenger seat. In all the years since the reservation came to be, amid all the people who had come and gone, amid all the change of seasons, the road was the one thing remaining the same. It was full of the same fears, and full of the same dangers. The road being the only constant was the thing allowing the people who traveled upon it to change. *How have I changed? Have I begun losing hope among people who are doing the same?* On the side, was a man dressed in a long sleeve shirt, boots and a reflective traffic worker vest pushing a shopping cart full of what Carson guessed were his belongings. He often staggered when he walked, and Carson guessed he stayed drunk. Strange how he always managed to turn around and wave to Carson when he passed, and it seemed he could peer right through the old glass of Carson's car into his soul. Carson believed the road allowed only those individuals who were open and willing to change to survive. He believed he had to assess his position in life each time he took the road to the city or heading back to the reservation. For all the dead, bloody carcasses laying upon either side of the road and for all the wanderers who drifted over it for whatever reasons, Carson wondered where the road would really take him. Pastor Jenkins always said how a blessing was on the way for those who truly believed in God. People on the reservation saw blessings like so many images in rap music or hit song videos; fortunes had to be tangible. In the mind of the people, blessings were in the form of riches, lottery winnings or a companion to spend the rest of one's life with. Carson hoped one day The Lord would reveal himself to the people as their life companion, bringing equal footing among the people in terms of their thinking.

"May I see your identification please," the guard at the gate before the city asked with a stiff, outstretched arm. His hand was balled into a fist. "I recognize you, but you understand this is just routine."

"Of course," Carson replied, happy he finally received some sort of warmth from anyone on the city.

"You know what to do- please come in contact with no one," he instructed, opening his fist and instructing Carson to pass.

Another Monday and Carson stood alone again under the buildings and upon the streets in the light of day, wearing his sign. The people of the city rushed and walked by as if on fast forward, yet Carson did not feel so invisible as in days past. His mind's eye still saw Ronnie standing beside him, looking up at him and smiling. His son was proud of how his daddy came forth to the church and said what was on his heart.

"You did a great job yesterday, sir," a voice from behind Carson said. He turned to see the white man who was within the pulpit before he came out. His name was Bill Wilson, and he was a friend of Pastor Jenkins, which was the way he got into the pulpit as a guest. Carson did not trust him.

"Thank you. Is there something I can do for you Mister Wilson?"

"Actually, it's more like what can I do for you," he replied. "What would you say if I said I could get you preaching on the city channel? You could be broadcast into the reservation and beyond- have more of an impact. What do you think?"

"What I care about is the welfare of the people on the reservation!" Carson shot back. "Not becoming famous! Things are not well there- you can see that for yourself Mister Wilson!"

"Yes, yes I can see, which is why I am telling you about this opportunity. Instead of your message being sequestered in the church on the reservation and nowhere else, you could be broadcast on the city channel- think of how many more people you could reach!"

"What would I have to do to get this opportunity?"

"Just continue to bring outstanding sermons at your church, is all. Come make a proposal to the people in charge here in the city, I will make the appointment for you- please do it!"

"I'll pray on it sir, and get back to you soon." Mr. Wilson turned and walked away, without another word.

A fight began in a hall of Redemption High among two boys. Vince knew neither of them.

"I will go upside yo' black head!" one yelled.

"You just as black as me fool! C'mon with it then!!" the other screamed back.

The two were surrounded by other students looking to get a close shot of the action which would later serve as fodder for the cafeteria lunch tables. In the heat of their battle, profanities of "black this" and "black that" spewed from their frothing mouths toward one another, as if rabies had driven them both insane. They both then became focused in a physical attempt to tear one another's clothes off, and the closer they came to doing so, the more bloodthirsty the crowd around them became. Vince stood stunned at the level of pure hatred between the two, thinking it abnormal, even animated. Only an altercation with his father could even come close to evoking that kind of emotion from him.

The impression of the two crazed young fighters carved an image into Vince's mind for all the rest of the day, even while he had lunch with Olivia. After the last of classes ended, Vince walked Olivia to the side of the school before she began her walk home and shared a quiet moment before football practice began that ended with a kiss goodbye. In the locker room, as Vince got dressed for practice, Mike Chambers came up behind him, which caught Vince off guard. He was certain he finally had something to say about what happened on the practice field before.

"I want to congratulate you on a job well done, man," he said, extending his hand.

"W-what are you talkin' about?" Vince asked, reluctantly shaking his hand.

"I'm talkin' about that girlfriend of yours!" Mike exclaimed. "How a dweeb like you got a girl like her, I'll never know!"

"Hey man!" Vince snapped.

"Naw, relax, I'm just kiddin!" he said, slapping Vince on the arm. Way to go, man, seriously!"

"T-thanks!" Vince said, not really knowing what to say. "Mike, man, I didn't mean to.."

"I know, we got on you kinda hard that day!" he said. "At least you tried, man! At least you tried!"

Wow. As Vince watched Mike walk away, he began thinking maybe the guy was not that bad after all.

SIXTEEN

"HILL! WHAT IN THE world is wrong with you son?!" Coach Turk yelled. "You got the size, speed, and strength, but you're just not aggressive enough son!"

"Yes sir, I'll try harder sir!" Vince responded.

"I can only put my best players out there, son, and you have the ability to be one of them!" he yelled. "I wanna make an All American outta you!" he wagged his finger at Vince's face through the facemask on his helmet.

"Yes, sir!"

"To be an All-American, son, you can't be out there thinkin' about how you're gonna move yo' arm, or what side of your butt goes first!"

"No sir, I mean, yes sir!"

"You gotta attack the ball!"

"Yes sir! My fault, sir!"

"And you know what I hate the most?" Coach Turk asked. "After you make a mistake, you have a habit of sayin' 'My fault!' 'My fault, coach!' Hell, everybody around knows it's yo' fault, you don't have to tell me that!"

"Yes, sir!"

"I'm lookin' fo' you to put up another fight, son! Put up a fight!'"

"Yes sir!"

"Or you won't play on my team!"

"Yes sir!"

As Redemption's football team rode on the bus to play their hated city rival Burke for the first game of the season, everybody hooped and hollered, yelling kill this and kill that which was their way of getting psyched up. Vince sat in the middle of it all, tired of being yelled at in practice, and anywhere else Coach Turk saw him. Vince had a feeling whatever he did, even if it was the right thing, the abuse was never going to end. Coach never said when Vince did anything right, only what he did wrong. As the team pulled into Burke High School's stadium, Vince had no idea how anyone else on the team really felt, and in the middle of the testosterone fest, he was afraid to ask.

At one point of the game, Vince made a crucial mistake on the field, and Coach Turk called him to the sideline.

"Son, you are stupid, and awkward, ya' ain't got no brain an' I always have to tell you what ta' do!" He yelled. "For all the time we sat watchin' film on this team, you still don't know nothin'!" Coach Turk would never admit he missed something. He was wrong and Vince knew it else why would he blame a sixteen-year-old for everything? Vince was afraid of how Coach had taken it upon himself somewhere to tell everyone he knew how he felt about him. *See that boy right there everybody? I'm tryin' ta' make him an All-American and he don't want it! He don't want it!! Kids today, God Allmighty!!*

The fourth game of the season came, and it was against Tillman, another city rival even greater than Burke. Coach Turk had lost to them the previous three years. As the team waited to exit the bus, city people screamed all around the entrance to the stadium, holding up signs.

"Go back to the reservation!!"

"Poor little poor boys!"

"No Redemption here!"

"Go back to the ghetto!"

"Are you animals vaccinated?!"

"Got money?!"

The team began yelling things back out the windows, and Coach Turk did nothing to quell it, sensing the growing hatred might fire his team up. Vince sat silent, indifferent to any of it. He felt tired and a win or loss here was not going to change that. Coach Turk made no secret of his hate for Tillman, or city people.

"LOOK!" he yelled over the noise outside and pointed out the windows of the bus. "I want this game- understand! Today, we are gonna show this team and these uppity city people what we can do- IS THAT UNDERSTOOD?!"

"YES COACH!!"

Whenever Vince stood in his defensive position on the field, he never knew what was going on because he became scared, afraid to make even the slightest mistake. Before the game, Coach Turk criticized everything about him from his form to the way he wore his arm pads. Whenever Vince made a good defensive play, Coach only yelled, "Get back to the huddle!" Toward the end of the game, Vince made a critical error resulting in the opposing team gaining significant yardage and later scoring, leading to Redemption losing the game. The tirade Coach gave exceeded his own boundaries, and no one wanted to see he had been drinking, but Vince smelled it.

"I told you over and again, look for the fake handoff! You were right there in position to make a play! You never listened to a word I said! What am I gonna do with you!?"

He blamed Vince for everything. From the first day of spring practice, when he pulled him into his office and said he wanted to make an "All American" out of him, Vince had a fear of what he might do or say afterward. Vince just wanted to play, and Coach Turk never gave him a chance.

The next afternoon in the film room, Coach Turk's ridicule towards Vince knew no bounds.

"Everyone take a look at this- look at Hill, your *teammate!* He has no idea of where the ball is, nor does he even care! We are trying to be a championship team! We don't have time for that! This isn't a day care! Look at you up there! What are you tryin' ta' do? Find your girlfriend? She ain't out there! You spend too much time up her skirt Hill! You need to get down to playing the game of football, not chasin' around some flusy!"

"MY GIRL IS NOT A FLUSY! TAKE IT BACK!" Vince yelled, standing up from his chair.

"Hill! Sit down!" one of the assistant coaches yelled. "Sit down, NOW! Show that much fight on the field!"

"TAKE IT BACK!" Vince yelled.

"Who do you think you are, standing up in my meeting and yelling at me?!" Coach Turk said. "You want a piece of me, come on, I said your girl is a flusy- what are you gonna do about it?!"

"Why you-" Vince lunged at him and Coach ducked, came up from behind and punched Vince in the back of the neck, sending him to the floor.

"I want to see another fight out of you, but you ain't got another fight left in you!" Coach said.

"Get out of my sight! You need to hustle and find the football, son! What the hell is the matter with you? We go through this stuff in practice, and you don" listen to a word I say! I swear you are the dumbest boy I ever coached!"

"GO TO HELL!" Vince yelled, taking off his jersey and walking out of the room.

All of Vince's teammates sat silent as Coach Turk continued bombarding him with names.

"You're a quitter son! You'll always be a quitter! A loser, that's what you are! You'll never be anything in life but a sissy!"

The pain of constant ridicule in front of his teammates became too much for Vince to bear, and so with the season at the halfway point, he quit the team, but not without more pain and ridicule. The coach asked Vince into his office for one last parting shot.

"Son, you're a quitter, and you will always be a quitter," he said again, pointing his finger right in his face. "You'll be the type who will never want anything out of life, and you make me sick!" Vince believed him, just like he believed him when he said it was all right to hit Mike Chambers. "You think you can just walk away from all this? You think you can make a fool out of me by quitting? You won't get away with it! Get out!"

After Vince left the team, he was held in contempt for it by most everyone in school. Vince had displayed what they considered a sign of weakness. With his father, Vince knew the worst was yet to come.

"YOU QUIT TH' TEAM?!!!" David asked, shocked. "Why you- What Coach say that was so mean? You a sissy, a sissy little boy who gotta have ev'ry little thing his way!"

"Dad, he abused me every single day! I got tired of it! I didn't know how to tell you!"

"He got a hard job boy! Nobody say it was easy- if it was, ev'ry body be doin' it! At least take some time to think 'bout it!"

"*Think about it?!!* Dad, that guy is crazy! I don't ever wanna go back to play for him! He called Olivia a flusy!"

"You don't know her, maybe she is a little flusy, I don' know!"

"WHAT?!" Vince asked.

"Son, I want you to become…"

"Become what?" Vince asked. "An athlete student? It's "student athlete" and by the way, my grades are okay, not that you've noticed! This is all about you, isn't it? Dad, have you even heard a word I said? I don't think you have- this is about how you look- somebody to carry on your days as a player! Just 'cause you failed don't mean you gotta lay it all on me! You don't even care how I feel!"

"Feelins ain' got nothin' ta' do wit' football!" David shot back.

"Oh yeah? Well neither do I!"

After Vince told his father of his decision to stop playing, David had no more words of courtesy left in him, so he said nothing. He said nothing, day by day, to his own son. Nothing in the morning and nothing in the evening. To Vince, his father had became a different person, in truth, when he met Olivia. *I hope he does not think she is the reason why I wanted to stop playing. Why does everyone hate my girlfriend? If my father does not want to talk to me, whatever.*

Olivia remained steadfast by Vince's side, though she knew Vince had become unpopular, even among people he thought liked him. To her, it did not matter if Vince played sports or not. To her, what mattered was what was inside him and that he loved her.

On an afternoon when Vince would usually be at football practice, he walked through a barren field with his arms around Olivia.

"I think my father blames you for me quitting the team," Vince said.

"Me? Whatever," Olivia whispered. "Your dad did act kinda funny that morning we came for you. I told my mama about you Vince."

"You did?" he replied. "And, uh, don't tell me, she's mad because I decided to quit the team too?"

"Vince, that's not true, come on, you know I never ever cared whether you played or not- I care about you for *you!*" she pleaded. "My mom doesn't even know you- yet."

"Now you are one thing I'm sure of! Thanks for being around! I mean it!" Vince kissed Olivia like he had never kissed her before. He closed his eyes for those few moments and forgot everything and everybody on the plains.

"I want you to come over Saturday night to our place!" Olivia whispered. "I want you to meet mama."

"You want me to meet your mama?" Vince asked.

"Sure," Olivia replied. "You say that like you don't believe me!"

"I believe you," Vince said. *"I believe you."*

SEVENTEEN

"BORED TEENAGERS RUN back and forth across the dirt roads of the reservation vying for attention, daring passing vehicles in games of chicken every day. I fear the adults in our midst on the reservation- the ones who are challenged by the teenagers- the ones who have become so full of anger and venom, angry enough to pass their shattered perspectives on to their children so they might never know what a beautiful place the world can really be. I can see them- hurrying to or from some demeaning job in the city and running over one of the teenagers in a moment's notice on a bad day, with another parent then weighing the option to kill in a fit of rage while his or her child lay dead. Sometimes, I see small children stop for a moment to savor the sound of the bells of an ice cream truck whistling through the air, and the sound itself is almost as satisfying to them as the cold water from the plastic pistols touching their heated skin in summer. I can still remember a time when that sound meant as much to me as it does them now; a time when I did not have a care in the world. In my youth, time was only a thing standing still- a thing for my friends and I to play within before I had to, as I neared adulthood, equate it with money. I remember having no idea of what God was about then, though sometimes I wondered, as my friends shuffled their way home toward the setting sun, was something or some big nice person responsible for them, my parents and my home. Life was astonishing then just for the wonderment of it all, each and every day.

The high spirited scene inside our church belies the very outside world itself; people now stand all over the sanctuary, hands in the air, waving to an entity they cannot see but are becoming dead certain is there. In number, about a hundred and fifty people stand throughout the sanctuary. A hundred and fifty people is a good thing. There are so few of our numbers left, and most Sundays, when Pastor Jenkins was alive, fifty or sixty was the norm. Many times when I was a Deacon, I looked within the crowd behind me and some stood crying with eyes closed while others wrapped their own arms tightly around themselves in desperation.

'Is there anyone who needs a prayer?' Pastor Jenkins would always say. 'Please step forward.' Many times, no one came, though so many us were in need. I stood up from the front pew sometimes and looked behind me at the silence. Nothing- not loved ones dying, not shattered dreams or even hope- ever seemed to shake the people up. As I stared into blank faces pretending not to be affected by life itself, I wondered which of them I could turn to should I ever need someone besides The Lord. I was the youngest Deacon of them all, and I suppose I had some things to learn, namely what my purpose was in all this within the remains of those who were left on the plains- the harvest of the brokenhearted- the throng of those who still wait for a word concerning where their lives are going. For those who have come and gone, like my son, I stand unable to tell the collection of souls before me anything in the form of an answer. Life has reached the point for them where they do not want to hear scriptures anymore; they are just words on a page. Some of them are so young still- black youth left by their parents so desperate to maintain, or acquire, dignity in an outside world far away within the consciousness of their own fears. The youth are left now to wander on a stage of a life requiring answers, and I have none for them. Oh, how I wish I did. Perhaps this thing- being on the channel from the city before them in their homes can be a good thing. Perhaps they can become uncomfortable enough to take a look at themselves- that is my hope- and while they assess, begin to build a better world for their children. Thank you."

The room of people from the city's television channel applauded before Carson, and he hoped a new day on the reservation could begin. He decided to go to the city, to be broadcast back to the reservation and beyond.

Pastor's Diary- November 2050

Talk about being turned all around without a sense of self. There are times when I sat in this church all alone, with the lights off, realizing all at once I could be the biggest fool of them all. Those people out there in the rat race- the ones in the shirts and ties and the suits and the dresses and high heels and makeup- a great many of them don't even make an honest living, and here I am praying to someone or something that to now has not come by to even check on me- or maybe I have not been willing enough to see him. Many people outside these doors- money stands as their god, and money is all they will listen to. If the people on the city channel did not think I could make them any money why would they even bother with me? That is the real reason I suspect they welcomed me on the channel- become a celebrity to help peddle their wares to anyone who will listen, anyone who will buy, but I pray the Lord's message will win the people over despite all that. What chance do my people have if they cannot even learn from all the mistakes we have made in the past? As fools, we fight over what we think is a position of morality at a city man's dinner table, and we feed our children scraps from the scraps which have long gone stale. I fear my own people now-diluted, disillusioned, dumfounded and dazed. I can feel our time becoming more desperate by the day. Scavengers of hopes and dreams among our numbers grow more in number by the day, yet I will continue to pray. Do you hear me? I will continue to pray.

Driving along the road it happened again, I witnessed a tear in the vastness of space, like a ripped piece of paper. Through the tear, was another world, the kind of world where there was no drought in summertime and no frostbite in winter. Trees were healthy and green. Green grass stretched for miles over the plains and there were no bloody animal carcasses to be picked up from the road. I stopped my car and stood in the middle of a field of green. I was the person I used to be- a person who always had joy, and no real worries to speak of. Life was easy. What happened to me? Everything now is I, me and mine. A fault of mine is that eventually, I begin relying on myself after waiting on anything for any length of time, even if it be the promise of seeing The Lord. That is why I am the one who needs prayer the most.

EIGHTEEN

THE FOLLOWING RAINY SATURDAY night before Thanksgiving, David reluctantly drove Vince across the reservation in his ragged, smoking car so he could spend time with Olivia. Vince told him he was going to meet Olivia's mother, so there was no need to worry about the two of them getting into trouble.

"Dad, could you just let me out here? I'll walk the rest of the way," Vince asked, not wanting him to see Olivia at all.

"Why you wanna be let off here?" David replied, suspiciously. "It's raining. I'm hea' now, let me take you to th' door."

"Dad, please, just let me off here," Vince pleaded. "I just want to be let off here, thank you."

David was hesitant for a moment, looking at Vince without a sound as the rain beat down the roof of their old car. He finally gave in, and untied the rope holding the passenger door together. "I see you later," he said, trying with all his might to hide his disappointment at the thought of not seeing Olivia.

"Stay outta trouble!" David called through the window of the car as he drove off through wet mud. As the car limped away, Vince saw in the rear passenger seat a figure- hooded- it's dark open face staring back at him. When he closed his eyes and squinted again through the massive raindrops, the figure was gone.

"It's only the rain."

With blurred vision from the storm, Vince began walking through a small clutter of run-down shacks marked with grafffiti, careful to avoid broken glass laying within the trash and mud beneath his feet. Boys from Redemption High stood silent, smoking in a playground area nearby made up of a set of broken down swings, a sliding board and monkey bars. As small as the reservation was, the looks on their blank faces said they could not recollect ever seeing Vince. Even through the lighted beads of water filled the air, the strange smell of their smoke was everywhere.

"Number 256," Vince whispered to himself.

Vince knocked on a crimson door, where chips of paint had been painted over again. He looked to the left and right of the house, making sure no one followed him.

The door opened to Olivia, smiling. "Come on in," she said, pulling his arm.

"I'm glad to see you too," Vince said with water dripping from his face, grabbing her around the waist and pulling her to him. "Where's your mama?"

"She went to the store and you're wet!" Olivia whispered.

"Oh yeah? How long she gonna be gone?"

"'Bout ten, fifteen minutes more, I guess."

Vince kissed her, and ran his fingers through her hair. After Olivia got him a towel, she led him into the kitchen, a place where she could react quickly if her mother came through the door.

"Why do you wear a dress every day?" Vince asked.

"It's part of my religion, my mother and I are Presbyterians. Why? You don't like it?"

"I hate seeing your legs every single day, actually," Vince said sarcastically with a wry smile.

"Oh, I don't know," Olivia teased. "I think I have nice legs." She raised her dress all the way up to her thighs, and the sheer black stockings she wore sent Vince through the roof.

"I love you Olivia….so..much!" he panted, kissing her neck.

"OLIVIA!" it was her mother, at the door. The door of their apartment swung open and Vince could not hide how flustered he became when Olivia looked into his eyes and said she loved him too.

"Uh, mama, this is the boy I told you about-Vince Hill! Vince, this is my mama!"

"Pleased to meet you ma'am," Vince said, extending his hand.

Olivia's mother stood silent, taking in the fact she had come just before they were about to get into something they should not have, judging from the flustered looks on both their faces. "So, you're the boy who quit the football team?" she asked in a curt manner with her coat dripping wet and not offering Vince her hand in response.

"I am, I mean I did ma'am,…you see my coach was-"

"Oh you don't have to give me excuses about why you quit on them!" she snapped. "We need young men to step up around here, not be quitters! I just want to know are you gonna quit on my daughter the way you quit on them?"

"Ma'am, I-"

"Are you gonna quit on my daughter?!"

"No ma'am!"

"Do you do drugs?" she yelled.

"Absolutely not!"

"MAMA!" Olivia cut in.

"Baby, half if not all of these jokers out here are liars, and weed smokers, and all they wanna do is get under your dress!" Mrs. Henry screamed, getting in Olivia's face. "Your own father was one of them, out there! Instead of takin' care of his family the way he was supposed to, he quit on us! Walked out because he figured a life of runnin' the streets was mo' important! I'm not gon' let that happen to my daughter!" she growled, turning to Vince.

Vince turned back to Olivia. "I'll see you later!"

"Look at 'cha! Quittin' already!" her mother snapped again. Vince walked out into the rain and closed the door behind him.

Vince knew he had nowhere to go. His father was supposed to come back at a certain time and he had no money to call him. Besides, he was too angry to even speak. Instead, he sat out on the edge of the group of homes near the road, away from the dope smokers on the playground, but close enough to Olivia's building to think she just might come out, just for a moment. She never did. Vince watched the young men who were only a bit older than him, standing in clouds of smoke they recreated time and again by puffing on marijuana rolled in cigarette paper. Vince watched them pass a wet brown paper bag with a bottle of something inside from one hand to another, taking turns putting it up to their mouths. One of them pulled a hood over his head and for a moment, Vince was reminded of the figure he thought he saw in the back seat of his father's car. *The windows were just dirty, that's all.* Vince sat silent amid the oncoming traffic, waiting for his father to come back.

Later that night, Vince watched television with a sore spot in his heart over Olivia and the way her mother treated him. Unknown to him and within his anger, The Specter of Evil had found a way into their home and he stood beside Vince while he sat in darkness before the light of the television, waiting for just the right moment when he could console him.

"Son, don't worry 'bout it, I guess them things will happen," David consoled, wondering if he would ever get the chance to see Olivia again.

The modest television in Vince's room broadcasted several other weaker channels outside the city channel. Events and people on the other channels looked as if they lived out their lives inside raging snowstorms. On channel after channel, Vince saw how little the television had to offer him.

"What eva you wont me ta' do suh, jest let me know!" a black character said.
"That will be fine Rochester, have dinner prepared at seven-thirty, I should be back by then."
"Yassuh."

Click.

Look at him run the ball! That guy is so quick, wow! He's jumpin' around like a little monkey!
Click.

"Now, honey, you know that ain't how it really is! A man's gotta do what a man's gotta do and dammit, I'm a man!"

Click.

"Oh, kiss me, you fool! You dammed crazy fool!"

Once Vince turned to the city channel, the snowstorms disappeared, replaced by vivid colors and crystal clean, appealing sounds. Even within he and his father's modest abode, on their modest television, the channel presented its view in immaculate fashion.

"Informative news! The entertainment you love! Sports! This is the city channel, broadcasting to you from Washington D.C., The Country's Capital! Number One!!"

Mired in his anger and frustration over Olivia, Vince viewed a world in love with sports and mayhem. He felt invisible, no longer wanting any part of the football team at school. On most every day thereafter in his self-imposed exile, the tension between Vince and his father became unbearable. On Thanksgiving Day in their house, there was barely any food, barely any words, yet plenty of resentment. When Vince could no longer stand being around his father, he began staying after school to work out, alone. Even in the class he shared with Olivia, he had no words for her, disappointed at how she never came out that night to be with him. Vince's anger enveloped him, lumping Olivia into the category of "everybody else."

In his newfound, self-imposed exile, Vince saw billboards over the dirt roads, referring to products and places he knew nothing about. His black face belonged nowhere, outside of an arena. He remembered once with his father while at the church, a picture of a white man named Jesus over the place where The Pastor spoke. Who was he?

NINETEEN

As I sit before the congregation, I realize I no longer know who I am, walking on a path with no end, one in which I may indeed fail. Day by day, I tend to the needs of adults, many of whom never bothered to grow up, and they don't even have the courtesy to say thank you. When I serve, I cannot expect anything in return, not a hello and not even seeing them ask The Lord to come into their lives. I look around this church, at the congregation reaching upward to something or someone they cannot see, understanding all at once how many of our lives on this reservation and through the years before were cultured and grown on assembly line holograms which only boosted our narcissism and lack of self-esteem, yet face to face, each of us spoke a language to the contrary. Is it even right for me to once in a while think of myself-

this time about my sanity- all over again? In the years since I have been free of The Specter, I ask myself these same questions over and over. We search for the approval of city folks, still unaware of how we are not in their plans- except if you like fighting overseas or catching a ball. Ah, I remember those days of skipping down the sidewalk after some stalwart of society had patted me on the head, telling me I had done a good job, or that I was a great guy who never made waves. "Why, that's all I ever wanted sir," would always be my response. "I just want you to know you can trust me. When you can trust me, I can trust me too."

Lord, I try to comply, and yet, there are times when I don't even want to listen for your voice- that's how angry I get. I get mad enough to recite each morning that I am ready to become part of a larger wheel- a cog of a larger part bent on self-destruction. The wheel I am a part of does not even stand for what I stand for, but after a while, what does it matter? Better to go with the flow of the wheel than to stand alone and be crushed, huh man? I imagine standing side by side with thousands of people exactly like myself. On the surface, I want to believe I share mostly common goals, the same dreams, ideals and desires- knowing my own very existence was for the sole purpose of destroying the dreams of the guy next to me or better yet, just achieving my dreams before he achieves his.

As I sit watching the congregation while the music plays, thousands lay dead or dying on the outside, the same scenario as it has been for years. Guns, drugs, AIDS, the flood, ignorance, it's all the same now. What does it matter what is killing us if we never learn one itty bitty lesson from any of it? I am so tired and now truly uncertain if my life even has a purpose. I am the one most in need of prayer. I am a product of the physical and mental genocide among my people-a survivor- a truly malevolent creature in terms of a lack of compassion and Lord I ask your forgiveness. No wonder I started drinking, I was just looking for a way out, a place to hide, but I was wrong. I only succeeded in nearly destroying myself. After all those years of hiding I know now there is no place to hide, no reward waiting for me alongside The Specter of evil because he was and is a liar. When will be our time? When after we leave the doors of this church will the words that are spoken inside follow us out the door?

Carson stood, over a box containing the remains of a young child. She was killed on the side of the road by a speeding car within the reservation itself. She was only five years old. At the time she was killed, her mother was drunk, and in an attempt to pull her across the road in a hurry, they both got hit. Carson wondered if the mother wished she were dead already.

"The life of one so young, cut short. She is with God now. I pray that lessons will be learned here and that her life will not be in vain." For all the funerals Carson had ever been to, he finally realized they are for the living, not the dead. The living need reassurance of how the dead are going to a place of peace and tranquility, so that when their turn comes, they know they too can go to that place. As the mother began screaming in pain, Carson wondered if it crossed her mind that her pain came from the idea of perhaps she did not do all she could have for her child. All the hurrying, all the rushing around- just for another drink into an alternate, but temporary reality.

Long after the funeral was over, Carson stood back in his flat, in front of the dresser in his bedroom, looking up at the cross hanging on his wall. He was angry, but of late he was always angry. *Is that the best she could do for her little girl? Why is it that we as a people are always the last to know? Our inability to care for our young, not giving them the things they need to survive in this world like a simple sense of self, grates on me like fingernails scratching on a blackboard. How can we supply them something we ourselves never had?* All the crying and lamenting in the world would not bring that little girl back. All the anger Carson could muster would never bring back the part of his life he chose to simply throw into a trash can following The Specter. The question was which of our young was next to die on the roads in our attempts to escape our own self-hatred? Carson looked around his humble place- at his bed, at the small kitchen, at his color television gathering dust, at his cracked wall mirror and at all of the other little trinkets reminding him of how he was only a man standing on a vast, turning globe. There was his Bible, some old plates and many old books given to him by a thrift store. Half of the things in his place were from thrift stores. In silence, Carson remembered people who counseled him while he sought The Specter, keeping their fingers crossed over how his life might turn out for the better while he hauled around the idea of a pain free way away from what was reality. They only wanted to see Carson stand on two feet again, to see him walk sober in the land of the living, and they wanted to help in any way they could. Carson stood silent, still grateful. He remembered, as he began turning his life around, the day he got that color television for twenty-five dollars. It was a happy day, being able to afford another view out of the reservation besides soiled windows, even if that view was tainted. He could not remember the last time he turned it on.

"Daddy, c'mon, can I have some money?" Ronnie asked, tugging at Carson's shirt. "Daddy?"

"Oh, yeah, yeah, son," breaking Carson out of his trance. "What do you want?"

"The ice cream truck daddy!" The sound of the bells from the ice cream truck had made its' way to the corner, playing a happy tune.

"Yeah, what do you want? Never mind, here, get me something too- a cone- and do me a favor- don't give my change away like you did the last time!"

Ronnie ran away, over the dead grass of the small yard cracking beneath his little feet, money in hand. Carson realized he did not mind so much Ronnie giving the change away the last time he went to the ice cream truck. He gave two dollars and twenty-five cents to a kid who wanted something, but had no money. The truck began pulling off down the road until the driver saw Ronnie off to the side, his little legs carrying him as fast as he could go. He was only doing what Carson had taught him to do. The boy had a heart, and he was glad about it.

Once Ronnie and the other boys around the truck held cold treats in their hands, they began making their way back toward Carson when an old truck sped down the thoroughfare, scattering the boys to one side of the road in a cloud of dust. Carson balled his fists in anger, clenching his teeth.

TWENTY

AFTER A SHORT WHILE, the vision of the two fighters in the hall at school had almost vanished from Vince's memory when one night at home David decided to watch an "important" boxing match which came on television through the city channel. He did not care when Vince stopped doing homework as a lot of loud brouhaha on the television had caught his attention about how great the fight might be. The two participants were black; "Fast" Johnny Collins and Tyrone Watkins. When each of them made statements to the media, Vince noticed how each were surrounded by whites. It was the "handsome" Johnny Collins versus Watkins, who was not so handsome. It so happened Collins' skin color was of a lighter shade than Watkins', and as he addressed the television audience, he made frequent reference to that fact.

"That man is ugly!" Collins joked. "You hear me, U-G-L-Y and dumb! He belongs out there at the zoo, runnin' 'round with the apes! Eeek, eeek!" To further insult his opponent, he danced around with his arms hanging by his side, as if he were a monkey. The white people all around them stood laughing, and clapping their hands. Watkins only stood a short distance away, saying nothing.

David laughed at what Collins said too. David Hill, who was dark-skinned. Collins went through great pains to give the audience a point of view that since Watkins was darker in skin color, he lacked intelligence. Collins implied since Watkins was darker in skin color, he was closer in the evolutionary chain to being an "ape." As the fight drew closer, Collins, the more highly regarded fighter, suggested he would and should win, for the reason of being more handsome than his opponent, because of the lighter shade of his skin. Much attention had been paid even before this event to Collins, but to Vince, he spoke a foreign language when he talked about his opponent Watkins. The two men went through a period of exchanging more verbal profanities and even went as far as to call one another "ignorant." When they looked like they were going to come to blows outside of the ring, the program broke for commercial.

"Do you want to know when will be the next time you fall in love? How about when you'll get that new

job you've been dreaming about? Want to know your lucky numbers, and even when you'll hit the lottery? Call me- my name is Silas Cohen, and I'm a friend of the stars and disciple of the great Ravi Shankar, the man who influenced the Beatles! I have been sought after for advice by members of Congress about important deliberations, and even some past Presidents in matters of war and peace! I can get your lucky numbers- no problem! When is the next time you're gonna fall in love? Call me, I can tell you when! It's all in the stars!"

"I lost forty-two pounds with the North City diet, and for six payments of eight ninety-five, you can too! My social life is much better now! Here's how to order!"

"This is the most absorbent paper towel ever made! This is the only paper towel you're ever gonna need for the rest of your life! It's amazing, it's indestructible, it's affordable! Here's how to order!"

"It doesn't matter if your credit is good or bad- it doesn't matter how much money you owe- I can show you how to get rich! Own that house you've always dreamed of owning! Live the way you deserve to live! Order my book today!"

"Good evening folks, I am Pastor Carson of The Baptist Church of The Reservation. Has life got you down? With the help of Christ, I can help you turn it all *around! I will be coming to you on Sunday mornings in January, here on the City Channel. Until then, May God bless you."*

Vince wondered if Silas Cohen, an absorbent paper towel or Pastor Carson could actually tell him what was going to happen with Olivia and her mother, but he was in no mood or position to pay for anyone's advice. It had been almost two weeks since that Saturday night, and Olivia had not spoken to him since, disappointed he supposed, because he walked out. Once the fighting between Collins and Watkins began on the screen within the ring, the cheers grew louder with every blow, and their taunting of each other revealed a hatred. The ferocious vision of the two black boys fighting in the hall at the school superimposed the television screen Vince watched along with his father. Between the rounds, information came in commercials about caring for babies and sales at nearby grocery stores from a slew of "respected" citizens, black and white. Toward the end of the fight, many blows had been thrown, but Watkins had gotten the better of Collins. Finally, with one dull thud, Collins fell to the canvas after a big left handed punch from Watkins.

One had to lose, and only one could win, but Vince watched his father slump down in his chair, sad over Collins losing the match.

The very moment lunch period ended and just before the start of the next class, Vince was no longer certain he was in love with Olivia. He was but sixteen years of age and he still dreamed of being with her when they were apart, which he supposed was a sure sign of love. He remembered how most everywhere he went during school hours Olivia was beside him, and the moment they began being seen together, he felt like somebody important. In the past when he stood in football practice thinking of her, the yelling and screaming was always light years away. The looks of disgust Vince got in his English and history classes did not bother him as much anymore. *He's a big, dumb football player. What's he doing in this class- with us?* The ironic thing about Vince's relationship with Olivia was that he began playing ball to meet girls, besides trying to please his father. Olivia hardly ever mentioned sports whenever they were together.

"You're a quitter, and you'll always be a quitter!"

Vince walked up to Olivia and pleaded. "Why did she have to treat me like that?"

"Vince, she's just being protective of me, that's all!" Olivia said, taking his hand. "You saw the people around our house! We just left New York where it is no better! She's just tryin' to look out for me!"

"Look, do you love me, I mean, are we gonna see each other, even though I hate your mother, for Christmas we can-"

"You hate my mother?" Olivia asked, puzzled.

"Well, I don't like her, okay?" Vince corrected himself. "I mean, look at the way she treated me!"

"You *hate* my mother?!"

"I didn't mean to say 'hate,' I-"

"Vince, maybe we should not see each other for awhile, I mean, I can't love a guy who hates my mother!"

"Olivia! I didn't mean it!"

"Goodbye Vince!"

After Olivia left him groping in the hallway, Vince decided after a few minutes to go to his first class of Spanish early. Not having to practice football anymore after school gave him renewed vigor in his studies and just in time too, because he was on the brink of failing several classes out of simple sheer neglect. Miss Gabby had taken offense at Vince's very presence during the time he played football- the time he was failing her class. It seemed to her Vince represented some sort of unfair class system she could do nothing about except deal out little F's, which she knew had no real bearing on whether he played or not because Coach Turk would just get any grade changed anyway behind her back if it was an important player. Once Vince walked away from the team, she lightened her vicious stance toward him in front of the other students. She saw how Vince had begun taking some charge of his studies, and it pleased her. Football had taken up too much time, and Vince was glad it was all over.

"Hey punk!" A hand came around and slammed Vince to the wall. It was Mike Chambers, and three of his teammates. The four of them pinned Vince to the wall and Mike got right up in his face.

"Hey, guess what I have behind my back! DING!! Too late! What do we have for this loser? It's…a FIST! Ha, HA! Listen, uh, now that you're not on the team anymore, I suppose I can get my revenge on you now, huh quitter?"

Vince fought to speak between his teeth, livid. "I thought you said it was over, that things were cool?"

"I said it was cool because Coach Turk was protecting your butt!" he said. "Coach has been the only reason you didn't get a butt whippin' sooner! Now that he's not gonna protect ya' anymore, I'm gonna decide when and how I'm gonna get my revenge. If you say anything about this to anyone, we're gonna go after your girl!"

"You touch her and I swear to God, I'll kill you all," Vince said in a calm voice that frightened even himself. He looked directly into Mike's eyes, without even fighting to break free from his grasp. "No matter what you do to me, I swear, you better stay away from her."

"Ooh, I'm trembling!'" Mike joked, though he felt Vince was actually serious. "I'm gonna get you punk, when you least expect it!"

Mike and his teammates backed off, and Vince thought to go to the principal's office. *That won't do me any good.* They were star players, and nothing was going to happen to them. When Vince arrived at Spanish class early in a huff, he found his teacher Mrs. Whitney sitting alone within a row of the students' desks writing in a small book that looked like a diary. She wore a multi-colored dress with small mirrors made into the chest of it. It was sheer, long and flowing. From under the dress, a pair of tan boots donned her feet that looked expensive. She sat with her legs crossed, and between the dress and the top of one of her boots, was a tantalizing glimpse of her knee and the green stockings she wore. Mrs. Whitney dressed like no other teacher in the school, and Vince had noticed whenever she taught class how she was always so happy, so full of life. She was white and from the city, but Vince could feel in her teaching how she was a really nice lady, despite the terrible behavior of the class. As Vince took a seat near the back row of empty chairs to continue lamenting about Olivia, she began speaking.

"Hello, Vince," she said, in a whisper. "You're here early."

"Hi," Vince replied. Watching her write in her book, Vince remembered her touching his hand through offering help with a phrase in Spanish. Vince noticed that day how her hands were covered with chalk dust which later appeared on his pants and sleeves. Vince was afraid of her because she was always kind to him. Once in her class, he took a long look at her bright face as she was in the midst of instructing and saw faint lines of age around her bright green eyes. Her deep auburn hair made her look so unlike any woman he had ever seen, much less talk to. As unpopular as he had become for walking away from the team, Vince felt no one around school ever talked to him anymore without a string of ridicule being attached. Only bookworm girls from the corners of classrooms gave him the time of day, those with pigtails, bifocals and no sense of adventure- those who believed he was some kind of god just because he played a game. Vince thought whatever Mrs. Whitney might have to offer, he wanted no part of it. In fact, he got the impression she began talking to him, in her whispering tone, because she actually felt sorry for him. The faculty knew what Vince was going through, and some saw it as courageous, and told him so. Others just did not care.

"Taken a sudden interest in Spanish now have you?" Mrs. Whitney asked, looking down and writing something into a new book- a lesson plan book.

"Uh, yeah, uh, I just need a place to sit for a minute," Vince said softly. "Do you mind?"

Mrs. Whitney stopped writing and looked up at Vince, at first not saying anything. The look on her face was one of surprise. "No, no Vince, I don't mind, you can sit there."

"Thanks," Vince whispered.

She looked like she wanted to ask Vince questions about why he wanted to sit in her room, while Vince believed she could see how he was distraught, but she said nothing more.

After Vince dared leave the team, and after Olivia walked away, life for him became oppressive. He did not feel he could go to any of the places around school he knew his former teammates frequented. They held resentment toward him for committing what they saw as an act of treason. Vince could never make them understand how the things Coach Turk said hurt him. Words like "hurt" and "feelings" were never supposed to come up around "primal" people like football players, because they regarded all that as sissy stuff. After Vince stopped playing, he found there was not one single one of them he could talk to about anything. He had nothing more in common with them. The trouble was, they were everywhere, and school for him became one big hiding place.

While Olivia took her time in deciding what to do with him, Vince found himself going to Mrs.

Whitney's class early again and again. At first, he went to her room just to see if she would still be in that exact same chair. Then, it was to see if she would still be writing and then, to see if she would really mind his coming so often. She was there every time he ventured in and she never minded. At first, she would say hello, and they would not speak to one another again until the room was full of students and she was in the middle of her lesson. As they sat quiet in the beginning, Vince got an idea he might be invading her space, her quiet time.

"Mrs. Whitney, you can tell me the truth, does it bother you- me sitting here? I mean, I can leave you alone if you want," Vince said.

"No Vince, it doesn't bother me," she said in a courteous manner. Vince felt like what was a cold shrug from her as well.

Vince got up from the chair he was sitting in, in a huff. "It's no problem, I can leave you alone if you like, just say the word!"

"No Vince, honest, you don't bother me sitting there!"

"Then why do you seem so mad when I come in?" Vince asked. "I come here because everybody in school hates me, including my own girlfriend, and I thought this was the one place where I could come in and be quiet for a few minutes! If I'm bothering you though..!"

"Vince, I've heard about what you are going through, after quitting the team and all!" she said.

172

"That is why I never said anything. Yes, this is my quiet time, but I don't mind sharing it with you."

By the time she had finished talking, Vince was already beside the door, ready to walk out. "You know about me quitting the team?" Vince asked.

"Vince, everybody knows about it- you are popular, you know!" With that, she smiled, and Vince felt like he could trust her.

Christmas came and went without Olivia and still without much said between Vince and his father. Over the course of the weeks following Olivia walking away, Vince acquired a feeling Mrs. Whitney was even waiting for him in her room. Her room was a place where Vince could forget his worries.

"You know Vince, not every boy would have done what you did," Mrs. Whitney said as they shared a large orange she brought in from the city. "I thought it took real courage to do something like that, to go against the grain and be unpopular."

"Really?" Vince asked. "You think it took courage?"

"Yeah, I do," she replied. "I mean, look at that coach- he's still down there abusing those young boys and unfortunately, they don't know any better than to know they can just walk away, like you did."

"Courage, huh?" Vince sighed and looked out the window at the football field that could be seen from Mrs. Whitney's room. "I didn't feel like it took a whole lot of bravery to walk away from him. I hate him. All I know is I did not want to deal with him anymore. I like football, but I hate him. He took all the fun out of playing for me."

In the quiet time of nearly each and every day before classes began, before Mrs. Whitney's room became full of students asking questions and behaving badly, she and Vince began talking about everything. They talked about her and about him, his past with the team and the difficult present, and about his possible future. Vince was grateful of her being fully aware of the resentment following him, and in the beginning, after he said what he had to say about the team, she never asked about it again. Actually, Vince himself talked about so many things, the team never came up anymore. Her room was the one place, even away from home, where he felt he could go to someone who would listen.

Vince wanted to be with Mrs. Whitney all the time, and not just go to her room for solace. There was so much sincerity in her voice. Vince never received the kind of attention she gave him before from anyone.

The football season had ended, and as spring remained deadlocked in a perpetual battle to emerge from the infertile mud of the plains, Vince had gained no more friends, as the memories of most of the student body remained as fresh and crisp as a cold cucumber on a salad bar. "Quitter" became Vince's name behind his back, and the name eventually found its' way to his face. As long as he knew he had a friend like Mrs. Whitney, Vince no longer cared all that much. Speaking of Mrs. Whitney, Vince stood in the middle of a hall with her during a change of class, light years away from all the hostility still surrounding him. He became more surprised and excited each time he saw her. It never occurred to Vince of how little he began thinking of Olivia. Since the encounter with her mother, Vince's feelings for his girlfriend began fading like a distant memory, though she had went nowhere, still passing by in the halls, trying to decide what she was going to do with him.

"Ready?" Mrs. Whitney asked.

"Yeah, yeah, I'm ready," Vince replied. "Not that it matters but, where do you live? I mean, is it far, I- never mind."

"No, it's not far Vince," she said, smiling. "I live in the city. If you don't wanna-"

"I DO, I do wanna, wanna see your HOME!" Vince said, looking right into her eyes.

"Then away we go!" she said.

Most of the students had left the school either by bus or by walking to their homes, and most of the faculty had gone as well. Mrs. Whitney and Vince walked together on a short road where dying trees and many bare bushes fought for a gasp of spring. On the other side of the road, two lanes of spiteful rush hour traffic hissed and bellowed leaving school toward the gate. Vince began feeling exposed walking the short distance to Mrs. Whitney's car, perhaps because they looked so different, she and he. Cars with people inside them crawled by as Vince walked along with Mrs. Whitney, simply appearing to carry a box of odds and ends for her. He felt how every person in each vehicle was staring, examining the differences between them, the age difference- the color difference- and in his mind the obvious fact he held affection for her. Vince suddenly wanted to hide. He thought of his father, sitting slumped in a chair in the middle of a room at home and somehow he felt ashamed. In his mind, all eyes were upon him. All eyes were staring at him and laughing. Vince wished the two of them could just "appear" at her house, like magic, without ever having to deal with any part of a judgmental society.

Once they arrived at the city, Vince ducked down at the city's gate in the back passenger seat under cover while Mrs. Whitney showed the guards her identification. Mrs. Whitney drove her car onto a thoroughfare full of neon lights and billboards and an infinite number of shiny cars. People walked here and there, crossing streets and sidewalks, going into cobalt blue glass buildings and talking to each under green trees thriving in the sunshine. There were more people around the city in rush hour than he had ever seen on the reservation or even a football game. Many of them were dressed in suits, ties and carrying briefcases, looking important. He had caught glimpses of the city riding back and forth with the football team to games, but most of the people he saw from Mrs. Whitney's car window were white, with a few blacks sprinkled in here and there. The imposing stone buildings towered over Vince's head as he gaped from side to side while Mrs. Whitney seemed not fazed at all as she drove. She drove off the highway, went up a side street and arrived at a beautiful small wooden cottage amid many trees at the top of a secluded hill.

The place where Mrs. Whitney lived was on a one way street- a kind of exclusive area where if one did not live there, one really had no business being there. When Mrs. Whitney opened the door to her place, Vince walked into fruitful aromas, like cherry and oak. The floor of her living room was finished wood that shined and shimmered like water. Other parts of the floor were covered with Middle Eastern rugs bearing bold fringes on their edges. On top of a lovely fireplace sat old porcelain vases from the countries she and her husband had visited. Her kitchen consisted of many household appliances and smelled of exotic spices different from the simple salt and pepper of he and his father's dwelling. The two bedrooms in the cottage each held giant canopy beds with colorful bedspreads and pillows. Vince noticed on one table a pipe sitting in an ashtray over ashes. Suddenly from one of the bedrooms, two cats, a grey calico, and an Abyssinian, came out to inspect him. Vince had not yet said a word, but he believed the cats had sensed different footfalls upon the wooden floor. One side of her house was a screen enclosed, open air patio, which was where the two of them ended up drinking iced tea.

"Thank you for walking me to my car and coming home with me Vince," Mrs. Whitney said, smiling.

"Oh, it was my pleasure, I liked it," Vince replied. "Your house sure is pretty. Let's do it again sometime!"

"How about when I come back from vacation?" she asked.

"Uh, sure, sure," Vince replied, nodding. "You're going on vacation?" he asked, just grasping what she said. "Where? When?"

At that moment, Mrs. Whitney extended her hand to Vince and he took it. "I'm your friend, Vince."

"I know," he replied.

As the two of them continued drinking iced tea and talking, the early spring sun gave a chilly red salute from over the nearby hill, signaling the end of another day.

TWENTY-ONE

VINCE WAS HAPPY to finally receive a letter from Mrs. Whitney, as she opted to take a ten day vacation from school. During that time, the days moved in slow motion for Vince. Mike Chambers passed by with the same sneer and the same teammates who hung on his every word. Olivia passed by, still trying to figure out what she was going to do and the student body passed by without incident, without character, without impact. Vince's angst became strong during the brief time Mrs. Whitney vacationed, the time he was left to his own devices, without any distractions. He hated the feeling of apprehension that swept over him whenever he was alone then, like someone or something was always watching him.

Vince was not a very fond reader of the daily newspaper, except for the sports page, and it was there on a Sunday morning when he saw something that frightened him beyond belief. There was an article about a black man- a famous boxer who had just finished time in jail for raping a young black girl. When his sentence was finished, the public demanded he fight again, because of his great boxing skills, amid much fanfare. The article expressed some of the boxers' views, and Vince read how this man talked with pride about hurting people, and about how much he lived to hurt women while having sex with them, as if he was hurting an opponent in the ring. What scared Vince about what he read was how the "world" he lived in held the skills of this man in high regard, but it was of no importance to anyone how he needed help, or how the boxer held sick thoughts of hate bearing his own real pain. It was plain to see no one cared about *him*. For the sake of the entertainment he could provide, his personal issues were secondary. As great a fighter as he was, he was expendable in the sense that if he chose not to fight, society would find someone else to fill its needs for violence and mockery. What was even worse, he was the closest thing to a role model for any young black child on the reservation. Upon this realization, Vince wanted to shed tears, but he could not. He did not know what to do for his own self; his father had lost respect for him for walking away from the team and a madman while a girl he once loved walked around as if he no longer existed. The reservation was hooked into a giant entertainment console featuring rebellion, mayhem, violence and degradation. Their own degradation. Vince felt so much pain in a second, but he felt it more for everyone else around him because it was not even an instance of them being tricked or duped. Many on the plains had been and still remained quite willing to play a part in a circus side show. However, amid it all, Vince was diverted.

The moment Mrs. Whitney returned from her time away, she called Vince at *home*.

"I just wanted to hear your voice," she said.

"Yeah, I wanted to hear yours too," Vince whispered into the receiver with his father sitting nearby. "I'm glad you're back!"

"Come home with me tomorrow?" she asked.

"Great! Yes, I'll be there," Vince replied, trying not to get too excited because his father had begun watching him. He hung up the phone.

"Who *'dat*?" David asked.

"Olivia."

"Funny, it ain't sound like her 'da way you was talkin'," David replied, becoming excited at the very sound of her name. "Well, I guess you two back together, even after what you say 'bout her mama?"

"Uh, yeah," Vince lied.

Vince went to his room and lay on the bed. Weather permitting or not, he was going home with Mrs. Whitney. Just then, when he realized how much he really liked the woman he thought-what about the pipe in the ashtray in her home? What about her husband- I mean, did they sleep together? *Of course they sleep together- they're married!* Vince had never even seen the man. Even after coming to that conclusion, he was full of an excitement which transformed his life into something much more than just another adolescent going back and forth to school every day. School had more of a purpose then, if not to just go to Spanish class.

Vince set out with Mrs. Whitney after school again, under a cover of heavy, dark clouds rolling over the plains. The clouds seemed so close, Vince could reach up and actually touch them. There was not nearly as much traffic as the first time the two of them walked to her car.

"Many people have left town for the beaches- it's the Memorial Day weekend," Mrs. Whitney said.

"People must be somewhere else- the casino, working overtime or something else because the holidays don't matter much here," Vince explained.

"What do you mean the holidays don't matter?" Mrs. Whitney asked. "Vince, they matter everywhere to everyone."

"I don't think so," Vince said. "No one around here ever has any money."

"Vince- money is not everything!" Mrs. Whitney said, surprised. "There's your relationships with your relatives- the people who love you!"

"I told you, it's just me and my father, and he acts like he doesn't want to see me half the time since I quit the team."

"He's still mad over that? I mean, come on, you're his son for God's sake!"

"You tell *him*!"

Because there were virtually no cars or people around to stare at him, Vince allowed himself to feel free with Mrs. Whitney, even holding her hand for some moments. Yes, they were friends, and he was so glad she was back. Vince laughed without a care as she told stories of when she was on vacation in Europe. There was something about the dark clouds overhead as opposed to the sun shedding light on any and every thing it touched; Vince did not feel like the two of them were so out in the open, in fact, he felt like he was back in his room, and his best friend had just come to visit. Vince knew just how far they had to go that second time around, to get to that graveyard on the right taking them off Route Seven- the main path in the city- and onto the discreet, tree-laden side streets where he thought he might even try to put his arm around her. The moment they turned off the path, Vince decided to try.

"Did you miss me Mrs. Whitney?" he asked, in a playful way, placing his hand upon her shoulder. Vince really just wanted to see what she would say. He knew she liked him, but he wanted to find out just how much.

"Vince!" she responded, "of course I missed you- didn't you get my postcard?"

"Yeah, I got your *postcard*, telling me about all the places you were going, and the places you had been," Vince sighed. He was not in the mood to talk about postcards. "I mean, did you *miss* me?"

"Wh- yeah, Vince, I missed you- you're my friend!" she replied, as Vince's heart sank. "I had other friends I wrote also, who I missed as well."

A large knot developed in Vince's throat. Her words sounded so cordial, and so precise. "Did you miss me the most?"

"Oh, I see what you mean," she replied, touching Vince's shoulder in return. "Yeah, Vince, I missed you the most. Is that what you wanted to hear?"

"Yeah," Vince sighed. It really was not what he wanted to hear, but he did his best to pretend how it was. *I mean, did you miss me like a boyfriend?* Vince did not want to press the issue. It was right then and there Vince discovered he really liked his teacher. He wanted her for a *girlfriend.*

Mrs. Whitney did not say another word until they arrived at her cottage on the top of the hill. She checked her mail, put the key in the door, like before and upon entering Vince saw all the antique furniture and trinkets from the places in the world she had been in their same spots in which he left them last. The two cats she owned looked upon Vince with some curiosity from different angles of the living room, though not as much as the first time. Once the two of them witnessed their owner go about her business in the house, Vince had the seal of approval that quelled their curiosity toward trying to discern what his purpose in life was. In an instant, they went back to being live house ornaments. In the middle of Mrs. Whitney's dining room sat a gigantic table made of deep, dark, shimmering oak. Vince saw a distorted reflection of themselves upon its surface as they sat together eating a dinner of minute steaks, green peas and mineral water. Her style of cooking was different from that of his father; he had none. The firm peas on the plate in front of Vince had been lightly steamed. David Hill would have cooked them for a much longer time and added a little synthetic butter to them. Mrs. Whitney explained how she liked her fresh vegetables steamed to keep in the vitamins. As she talked, Vince thought of how the reservation sold vegetables in cans- at least those were what his father could afford. Mrs. Whitney sat *right* beside Vince at a corner of her huge table as they ate, but when Vince considered her politically correct answers on the way there, he began wondering what in the world he was doing there at all. Vince put down his knife and fork.

"Is something the matter, Vince?" Mrs. Whitney asked. Vince only looked down into his plate, really unable to speak for the pain he felt. He liked the woman. She was married.

Is something the matter, Vince? In that split second, the words played themselves over and over in his mind. Mrs. Whitney put her hand through Vince's thick hair and he turned to look directly into her green eyes. "Is something the matter, Vince? Don't you like your food?"

"Yeah, I like it just fine," Vince replied. "I like you, too, Mrs...I like you."

"I know, Vince," she whispered. "I know what you were trying to say when we were in the car. I *missed* you, I really did. Don't you know that already?"

Vince kept looking directly into her eyes, as her words scared him. They were exactly the words he wanted to hear.

"I feel good when I'm around you, like, I don't have to prove anything to anyone," Vince said.

Mrs. Whitney got up and cleared the plates from the table, and then went into the kitchen where she began fumbling with something inside her freezer. She returned with a lone scoop of chocolate ice cream, and two spoons.

Without a word, Vince picked up his spoon and began sharing the ice cream with her. As she looked down into her small glass dish, Vince noticed the light glaze of her auburn hair. He put his spoon down and ran his hand through her hair. Once he did, she tilted her head over to his touch. The moment Vince saw how she did not object, he put his arm around her neck and kissed her. Mrs. Whitney looked at Vince in surprise, without a word. Instead, she put both her arms around his shoulders and kissed him back, with a mouth full of chocolate ice cream.

Vince was afraid, more afraid than he had ever been of anything, including his father's anger. Everything had all been fun up to that point. He had enjoyed the conversations they had and coming to her home and all. Trying to kiss her crossed his mind, like something which would forever be impossible, simply because she was his teacher. Olivia was the first girl Vince had ever kissed, but kissing Mrs. Whitney was different from kissing Olivia. When Vince began kissing Olivia, the both of them sort of fumbled their way about each other, and sometimes their kisses were nothing short of just putting their lips together in the beginning. Mrs. Whitney knew just how to put her lips on Vince's, and her tongue even went into his mouth a little, which felt funny.

Olivia, bless her little heart, could not give Vince the "positive reinforcement" Mrs. Whitney could. Olivia did not have the means to shower him with gifts and tell him what a great person he was, something Vince had never experienced before from anyone.

"Please Vince, call me Katherine," Mrs. Whitney panted.

TWENTY-TWO

DUE TO TIME CONSTRAINTS, Olivia could not lay Vince down in a king size bed draped in many expensive, colorful linens and give all of her physical self, all the while whispering how much she was in love with him, not to mention age and financial constraints. Vince's girlfriend was sixteen with a mother who hated him and vice versa. *There it is, I don't like the woman.* While lying in Katherine's bed, it was easy to admit how yeah, he could not stand the woman and that problem seemed like, so *five months* ago. In Vince's mind, he remembered braving the bad weather to get to their house that night and how that act alone should have been enough to show them both how he cared for Olivia, but nope. He appeared at her door with a runny nose from the pouring rain, simply content to spend an evening of holding hands and fielding any questions she and her mother might have for him in a kinda sorta impromptu press conference public statement, since it was his first time meeting her. The first chance Mrs. Henry got, she stated her belief, based on the symptoms she could see, that Vince was on drugs.

Drugs, indeed. After the second visit to Mrs. Whit- uh, Katherine's house, Vince's new routine consisted of finishing school for the day and making a direct path to his secret friends' house via the back seat of her car, with no one ever knowing where he was, often returning home late.

"Boy, whea' you been?" David asked. "I want you ta' know I didn't make you no dinner, and I stop makin' it 'cause you never home no mo'. At least let me know you ain't comin'!"

David had no questions about where Vince went, because when he appeared back home he was always clean and nothing seemed out of order. He was gone all the time, so the better. He never had to really be bothered with him anymore. The quitter. Once he heard that some of the other boys on the football team walked away like his son did, he never budged. It never even occurred to him to trust Vince a little more.

David Hill was a man who never knew quite how to express his emotions, however, almost every night after Vince's second visit to Katherine's house, not one more plate of supper sat inside the stove waiting for his own son.

Katherine's husband owned a basketball which rolled out of a closet when she grabbed for a box on a shelf. She told Vince there was the edge of a college campus two blocks from where she lived. Vince saw the court as they drove in, and asked to go play with it, to which Katherine agreed. When Vince arrived at the court, he found at least twenty young black men on the court who were enclosed in a ten foot tall chain link fence glistening under the sun's light. Some of them were playing and some were waiting to play. Perhaps on the reservation, near Redemption High, it might have been a normal scene but to Vince, within the city amid a vast sea of whites, it was odd. While Vince waited to play he noticed many college students outside the fence passing by all around, going in different directions- singles, in pairs, in groups carrying books. Vince watched them carefully as they went by. They were oblivious to the scene on the court. Despite all the yelling the players made while they ran back and forth, not one of the students even looked in the direction of the game. Vince noticed too, upon many of the arms of those playing, a mark, or a burn. The burns had healed to form ugly abscesses in the shape of horseshoes, appearing much like cattle brands.

Within five minutes after getting his first chance to play, Vince had the ball and was in the middle of leading a fast break down the court-one of his teammates running on either side of him toward the basket. In a sudden, decisive movement, Vince pulled up to the side away from the break and hoisted a twenty-five foot jump shot, one he was very comfortable with. Vince had already made two jump shots before in the game, from which he gathered they knew he meant business and was not intimidated. He missed. After his missed shot, a short, muscular young black man came up to him in anger.

"You shoot that shot again," he hissed through short breaths, "I'm going to tear your damn head off!" His arm bore the cattle brand Vince saw almost from the moment he arrived at the court.

"You don't own this court you jerk!" Vince snapped.

Once Vince made his response, many other young black men with the same cattle brand on their arms gathered around him. "Go your own way," another of them with excessive grease in his hair said. At that split second, under gathering clouds, Vince realized he could get into a fight with several blacks in front of hundreds of whites. He walked away with the ball, leaving them alone. Another who waited on the bench replaced Vince and they went on as if he was not even there. They even started over, erasing his points. It was all clear then, from the two fighting in the hallway at Redemption to the basketball court, enclosed within a fence. The basketball game was more than just a game. It was actually a process of elimination, one in which Vince was spared for the moment. Walking away and leaving the noise of the game behind, he would never forget about them, or the anger on their faces which appeared so different in a sea of white.

Early one evening after school at Katherine's cottage, the red orange sun sat on the horizon over a small part of the graveyard which could be seen from the patio window. The days were getting longer with the trees, the manicured streets, the parked cars and all of the houses being blanketed in red by eight o' clock. On one side of Vince on a small wooden table sat a glass of iced tea, complete with a slice of lemon. The glass had become chilled from the ice within, with condensation running down its sides onto a coaster underneath it. On the other side of him sat Katherine reading a magazine. In front of him, the television news blared about a black criminal from the reservation who had shot and killed four people in a local city restaurant. In an attempt to reform him, the man had been given a job in the city, but he shot them for the reason of wanting money out of the safe and in getting it, he decided to leave no witnesses. All the people who he shot and killed were black as well, from the reservation. Stories of the shooting victims surfaced within the story itself; a teacher who had been married for twenty-nine years who dedicated her life to helping children, a man engaged to a woman who had just given birth to their new baby boy, and two young girls named Maria and Anna who had just finished high school. With the help of the government, the two of them were about to attend a local city college. *I knew them both.* Katherine got up and left the room. The bad news was interrupted by a commercial trying to capitalize on an old rock music hit- "Nights in White Satin-" which had nothing to do with the product being sold. Vince quietly watched it all, the death, juxtaposed with the selling in between.

"I promise you, this is the last broom you will ever need. Get out your credit card, here's how to order!"

And now, a moment from Pastor Frank Carson of The Baptist Church of The Reservation:

"Many of us here on earth believe in The Lord Jesus Christ, and now it is time for us to begin acting like it."

"I remember that guy," Vince thought.

"We say we are all God's children but nothing we do makes sense anymore- the violence between ourselves, be it here in the city or on the reservation. It is the fear of one another which keeps us in bondage and a

perverse love of money taking our attention away from The Lord. There is a better way of life for you and for me. Join me on Sundays, here on the City Channel. Remember, there is power in prayer."

"Hey people out there- are you struggling with being overweight? I lost one hundred and forty-two pounds with The Eliminator! Go ahead, get in the best shape of your life for two easy payments of twenty-nine ninety-nine! Call now!"

Prayer. In a world where anything having meaning usually meant being tangible, "prayer" was like a phantom word that came in one ear and out the other. Vince remembered Olivia again. He saw her in his mind, alongside this man, this preacher she believed in, happily banging her drums for the promise of "a better life and eternal joy," she called it. She had probably moved on without him. Sitting in a velvet upholstered chair, Vince wondered whether she thought of him at all anymore. The thought of Olivia passed through his mind in a millisecond. He saw the violence, understood it and was even angered by it all. After Katherine came back out to the living room having shed all but her underwear and sat in his lap with a glass of wine to share however, she became the focal point of the universe.

The following Sunday, Vince stayed home, because Katherine had a function to attend with her neighbors. Sitting outside amongst the trash and rusted old car parts throughout his father's yard, he realized how everything with Katherine had happened so fast, and he barely had a chance to assess his life away from her. His father's house was a place where Vince no longer wanted to be. How could he compare old, dirty tires sitting in the middle of a dusty yard to a shimmering wood floor? How could he compare the sweet aromas of jasmine and cherry to the odor of dirt, mud and half washed clothes? How could he compare the warmth Katherine showed him every time they got together to the cold shoulder of his father? How could he compare the freedom of being with Katherine to the massive crab bucket which was the reservation? Yet, as Vince sat out in the back yard, watching his father go about in the shanty, he had a feeling he was wrong. Later that morning, he heard two neighbors standing nearby at the fence separating their two yards, talking about how they hated living next to other blacks.

"They keep their places run down," was one reason.

"They're too nosy," was another.

"They never help one another or aspire to do anything," was the overall gist of the attack.

Vince let the noise they uttered pass by him like the wind, flying away through the dying trees with the rest of the dirty birds ransacking the trashcans against fences of back yards throughout the plains. Vince lived in pure anticipation of when he would and could see his secret friend again. In school when he sat in Katherine's class, it did not feel the same because she had to give attention to others. The whole time in her class, it always felt as if they were not together, because she was great at not giving herself, or him, away. Meanwhile, Vince saw Olivia around in school from afar then, and he even sat away from her in class. Even Mrs. Gabby sensed something was different between the two. Vince saw Olivia being admired by the vultures in school who had been waiting for his emotional carcass to fall by her wayside, and it mattered not.

Vince experienced no emotions whatsoever as he looked upon scene after scene in the hallways of Olivia being courted by others. Vince learned quickly at his young age how one of the best things about any romance is the opportunity to tell someone else what is going on- to tell about how exciting it is, and what it is like to be in love. He realized however, sitting in the back row of desks watching the rest of the students file into Katherine's class, how no one could know where he spent his days after school. The more time Vince spent with her, the more he felt himself losing contact with people his own age- what their world was like, what their concerns were, the things they said to each other, and the things they liked to do. Vince did not even mind when late one afternoon, school was over and the guy who replaced him on the team rode by in a car with Olivia.

One day, as school ended, Vince waited out front beside the long line of buses full of students and ready to depart the school. He sat on the front steps of Redemption, completely out of touch with the boys his age jousting for position amongst themselves so they could see themselves better, never mind the girls. At the right time, Vince thought, he would dash to meet Katherine. At the moment he got up to meet her, he saw Olivia looking at him through a bus window, within a crowd, but alone. She looked as alone as Vince felt the day she walked away from him over her mother. *Anyone else got a mother problem?* There was no longer a conflict about her mother, or anyone else's parent for that matter, including his own father. Instead, he could not wait to spend the late afternoon with Katherine eating steaks cooked medium rare instead of past the point of well done. A little bit of juice was actually okay. He saw the vegetables on the plate in his mind- steamed and crispy. All that would be accompanied by cold, carbonated mineral water and perhaps a glass of Sauternes for dessert. Well, actually, dessert was covered. But the wines, ah yes, the *wines*. A chewy Cabernet, or a spicy Shiraz with the steaks. Perhaps a tart Sauvignon Blanc, or a sweet Riesling if she decided to prepare chicken or some fish. If they're feeling really lazy, a buttery Chardonnay would do, out on the screen-enclosed porch of the cottage where Vince looked so forward to altering his surroundings with her, before the sun set itself behind the tombstones of the graveyard at the bottom of the hill.

Before summer came to blaze upon already sparse blades of yellow grass, the school year was almost over. Katherine suggested to Vince, in bed, he should apply for college. College? It occurred to Vince then how he really had no other idea of what to do with himself other than drink with Katherine.

TWENTY-THREE

Pastor's diary-May 2051

FOR MONTHS, *As I have gone back and forth between the city and the reservation, I finally gathered the fact of how I know no one and no one knows me. I am as lonesome as a man can be, in this world I care for that does not care for me in return. It hurts to be alone. On the edge of the road each day as I pass, stands The Specter, cloaked within the shadow and gloom of night off to the side of my headlights, offering his leathery hand once again in friendship.* Come, you do not have to endure the ways of people. I will care for you. Come with me, and I will see to it you never feel lonely again. I told you how people cannot be trusted….they cannot be trusted! *This feeling of isolation I have is the very reason I served The Specter at all. I was afraid, so afraid if I opened my heart and cared for people, there was a chance I would be rejected. I worked very hard to never know what that felt like, hiding in the shadows of life and never taking chances. I realize now, on this road, each day I have is nothing but a spiritual reprieve. I must continue to believe the people here are good people. And if I do happen to be the vehicle through by which they become saved, what then? Is there no reward for this? When my wife passed away from this life, there was no reward. When my son passed away from this life, there was no reward. All I am left with now are people who believe in the tangible- money and only money. This place, the plains, are so foreign to me now. The violence and degradation has taken a toll on my soul. My only intention with the broadcast on Sundays was to reach more people, but the attendance at the church has not increased any at all. What does it matter anymore? I am now paid well for my service in the city and as I travel this long road in my new car, I can feel the reservation sucking the life out of me with all its ignorance and all its hatred and unwillingness, against this new car smell. Once I appeared on the city channel, I expected a welcome at the church which could have signaled a new beginning. I arrive now, to an empty place in either direction. No one to love now. Would it be nice to have someone to share this journey with, because the city is so cold? Perhaps. People there live next to one another, on top of one another, in front and behind one another without a word of greeting. I am broadcast, in the middle of the night, in between commercials for exercise equipment, hot tubs, and various inventions meant to make life for those who can afford to spend the money, easier.*

I walk the streets in the dark of night, without a word. I walk through crowds, without a word. No hello, no goodbye, no concern, no empathy, no compassion, no love.

"Hello Pastor Carson. Are you ready?"

"Yes."

"five, four, three, two, one."

"And now, a word from Pastor Frank Carson from The Baptist Church of The Reservation."

"Before I begin tonight, I would like to express sympathy for the victims of the horrendous shooting last week." Carson put down his glasses and looked directly into the camera. "You know, sometimes you might have things all prepared-right down to the hand gestures and then once you get ready to give that presentation, The Lord leads you in another direction. Any of you out there know what I mean? Ahem…Two of those victims, young Maria and Anna, were very close to me…..There are things in this world I will never understand. I will never understand how a decent man can marry the woman of his dreams, start a new family and before his newborn son even gets a chance to see and remember his face, he is shot dead. I will never understand how a woman who had been a teacher all her life, dedicating herself to the betterment of children everywhere- herself a conduit for young people toward a better way of life, can be cut down in still what is the prime of her life. I will never understand how two young people as respectful as the ones I knew who were working in that store- doing the right thing…..they were where they were supposed to be- CAN'T ANYONE OUT THERE UNDERSTAND? THEY WERE WHERE THEY WERE….SUPPOSED TO BE….DOING WHAT THEY SHOULD HAVE BEEN…DOING…..MY SON, RONNIE…WAS SO YOUNG…WHAT DID HE DO TO ANYONE? IS THIS THE THANKS I GET?!! IS THIS THE THANKS I GET?!!"

In an instant looking into the camera, Carson's mind went blank. He wiped away tears to see and feel The Specter standing in the broadcast room across from him. *Come with me and you will never have to shed tears again. I will always appreciate your hard work- I understand.* "I WILL NEVER COME WITH YOU!! NEVER!! YOU CAN'T MAKE ME!!" Carson shouted.

"Pastor Carson…Pastor, are you all right?!" the technician in the studio asked. Carson was alone in the room. The Specter was not there.

"Sir, we went to commercial," the technician said.

TWENTY-FOUR

OLIVIA PASSED VINCE BY over and over in the halls of school completely unable to understand what it was rendering him without the urgent need he always displayed to be alongside her. She feared the light for her was gone from his eyes for good. One day after geometry class, she grabbed Vince's arm and pulled him to her.

"I want to be with you- let me," she whispered. Vince nodded yes, but could not say a word to her. Olivia stood silent, watching Vince walk away as if he heard not one word she said.

David Hill sat sprawled out drunk in the middle of his simple dwelling watching television, at the mercy of whatever came on the channel, a puppet of some board room pencil pusher who never even met him. Drinking and watching television was all he ever did anymore, since Vince quit the team. As long as his boy played, David believed he had something to look forward to- Vince going on to turn professional and getting his father off the hook for being a *complete* failure, perhaps. When Vince came through the door and said he no longer wanted to play football anymore, David felt as if someone had snatched a winning lottery ticket out of his hands. A ticket taking him far from the reservation. *Where eva' I go, here I is.* At first, he was able to keep somewhat of a wrap on his liquid transgressions, but it was no longer necessary since Vince never came home anymore. Be it sports, dancing, complete foolishness, or commercials peddling products not using anyone close to his likeness or even taking into consideration his lowly financial status, it mattered not. If a point of view came through the television, David figured it had to be true or at least have some truth to it. *Yeah, sho', why not?* The Specter stood within the darkness of the shanty as its few windows to the outside world were covered with makeshift shades ranging from cardboard to old curtains to sheets. Outside, there was not a cloud in the sky, as life continued to pass David by. The thing watched David intently with its mildewed hand which never had the benefit of the light of the sun touching the worn chair near his shoulder. The Specter prepared David's heart and erased his conscience for the act of evil about to come. In his perpetually drunken, stagnant state, David became a slave to the lights and the pictures-the pretty, flickering lights coming through the tube. He imagined himself within the picture as someone important before he always passed out from the cheap, strong booze, but more as someone who was admired. He wanted so much to be admired. Yes, he had let go of his habit of drugs from the past, but The Specter was able to distort his vision again, blocking a feeling or longing for a life other than a mundane existence. As an odor of sour grapes filled the room, David preferred to avoid everyone, slinking down in his chair further. *Less trouble, who needs 'em?* He wanted to focus on the idea of being someone in the eyes of other men, rather than someone who went unnoticed picking up trash in the city for a pittance. David was one of the ones who took the bus to the city everyday to work because he could not afford to drive, but that day, he chose not to. It would not be long before the bright noon summer sun outside was close to touching the horizon with its finger and once it did, it would be the queue of how David had chosen to waste another day and yet another opportunity to be a father. Knowing that, David's anger grew. He was a failure, choosing a self imposed exile from all around him as a result of his fear of living. Besides, it was easier to just live in his mind because it took no real work. No buses had to be caught and he was tired of hearing about having to peel back and examine the onion of his soul to be able to live in his own skin. No one would ever have to oppose or disagree with him in his mind. If only he could turn back the arms of time; arms to console him once he realized how he was just a listless recollection of a broken spirit. A knock came at the door.

"I know that ain't Vince," he mumbled to himself. "He's never home no mo'."

When David opened the door to the midday sun, his sluggish spirit disappeared and was replaced with a sudden vigor he had not felt in years. His heart dropped to his stomach. It was Olivia, wearing an old knee length tuxedo black dress her mother gave her a time before for her father's funeral. She wore no slip underneath it and the dress might as well have been a cocktail dress from the casino for all David cared. Her dark, long hair was moist from walking under the sun yet styled and combed to the side, accentuating her fair skin and dark brown eyes. As she stood in the doorway, the bright, hot sun shone behind her sheer dress, giving David a voyeur's view of her entire body. Her shapely young legs were bare and silky as she wore light black slippers. Her arms were covered with sheer sleeves which appeared like stockings. She had even taken her glasses off, in one big attempt to get Vince back.

"HEL-LO! IS VINCE HERE?" She yelled, for the third time.

"He be back ina minute," David lied while extending his hand. "Come on in, young lady, make yo-self comfa-ble."

She reluctantly took his hand and came through the door, went over to a chair and sat down. As Olivia sat down, her dress flipped up to her waist and David caught every moment of it.

"How you get here?" David asked in his most polite tone.

"*I walked*," she replied, suddenly perceiving an odor of drunkenness about him. The mistake she made of coming through the door hit her in a wave. "W-When did you say Vince was coming back?"

"Should be any time," David replied. "I sent him to th' sto' over by the way for some little things. Girl, whea' yo mama at?"

"I-I-I'm glad you and Vince are speaking again....she's at *work*, why?" Olivia snapped.

"So she don' know you here den?" David asked, smiling. All Olivia saw when she looked at him was someone she did not trust, even though she loved Vince. His yellow smile of missing teeth, the way his hand caressed the chair he sat in while he looked at her and the seedy way his glossy eyes seemed to be measuring her.

"Ohmigod, uh, if you don't mind, I would like to wait out-SIDE!," Olivia said, getting up.

David popped up from his chair and touched her arm with his hard, cracked, weather beaten hand. Her skin was *so* soft. "Please, don' leave, I don' mean nothing by lookin' at 'cha," he said, laying his whole hand upon her shoulder.

"Please!" Olivia pleaded. "I just would like to wait outside!"

"I apologize baby!" David said, grabbing her by the waist.

"I'm not your *baby!* Oh God, TAKE YOUR HANDS OFF ME!" Olivia cried.

"Whas' wrong with lil' girls like you?" David demanded, his apologetic tone disappearing into a morbid, stinking calm. He blocked the door and shook his head from side to side in disappointment, all the while looking her up and down. "Why gals like you- pretty gals like you- gotta act like crazy- so STUCK UP!"

"Wha- I'm sorry! I'm sorry, please, please let me go, I didn't mean anything," Olivia cried, wiping away tears. "I didn't mean to make you mad, sir!"

"Well you make me mad!" David snapped in a low, sluggish voice. Her tears gave him complete control of the situation. "You *so* pretty!"

"Oh God! Thank you, thank you," Olivia replied, shivering. "P-please let me go, sir, I won't tell Vince, I won't tell nobody!"

"You damn right you ain't gal! I'm gonna kiss you now, ya' hear? All I wont is a little kiss, that's all! I ain't gon' hurt cha'!"

Olivia backed away, losing one of her slippers. "Oh my Lord, HELP ME! Please don't! Please!"

TWENTY-FIVE

VINCE WAS AMAZED at the fact he had gone so long without even the thought of touching Olivia, as beautiful as she was. He instead opted to be with a woman whom he could not even be seen in public with for her fear of someone seeing and recognizing her, and their affection for one another.

And so, to protect Katherine, Vince Hill chose to forgo the comfort of his own room for a prison of cooked meals, alcohol and sex. Perhaps he should not use the word "prison." No one ever once told Vince he *had* to be with Katherine out a life and death situation. Besides, how can a pole-vaulter pole vault with a *rope*? Vince was seventeen and in a situation where every move he made had to be calculated to the last closing of a door for Katherine's sake. She said she loved him, and Vince believed her. No one, besides Olivia, had ever told him that before.

To everyone at school who had ever noticed him, Vince had become silent and withdrawn. Without knowing, as he concentrated only on the growing affection between he and Katherine, a new derogatory name found its way about him; snob. Those same students who were content to label him a traitor became annoyed at how Vince showed no interest whatsoever in anything they did. The math club, the wrestling club, the reservation student union. As far as Vince was concerned, who needed any of that stuff. To him, those pursuits were just titles for anyone in love with the sound of his own name.

How does one seventeen year old explain to another seventeen year old he is sleeping with his teacher? His *TEACHER!* Vince knew no one he could really trust and after all, at his age, part of having a girlfriend as special as Mrs. Whit- uh, Katherine, was the opportunity to tell someone. Anyone at all- just to let someone know of how special Katherine thought he was, and what it was like to put his arms around a woman twice his age and actually kiss her. Vince knew of no one who eventually would not be able to resist going off into the halls of school blabbing about how "Vince Hill is making out with his teacher- ooo yuk, ohmigod, no he didn't, deg on, oh snap!" Vince suspected how as soon as his true opinion about something going on in the world might rub any hypothetical friend the wrong way, the proverbial cat would be out of the imaginary bag, so to speak. Even worse, he knew once he might tell someone, he would become an indentured servant for the rest of his time at Redemption, doing favors like bringing lunches, or even tutoring- like he could help someone with their math homework, right. Well, maybe. He guarded his secret friendship with Katherine like a hungry Rottweiler guarding a bone, suspecting she would lose her job if he did not. Vince began spending so much time with her, she became his world above all else. No one he knew would understand what it was like to be loved by a woman as wonderful and beautiful as Katherine. He felt like someone when he was with her, like he belonged in the world- not some wayward kid full of angst leading a hopeless life on a crappy reservation.

There were times when Vince daydreamed about the idea of everyone in school knowing how he and Katherine felt about each other. All of the students would just accept their being together, and that's just the way it was. Vince could walk into her classroom anytime he wanted and give her a kiss in front of students, faculty, whomever. Everyone would say, "Oh, that's just Mrs. Whitney's boyfriend Vince- he's cool. He's a traitor for quitting the team, don't get us wrong, but hey, no one's perfect!" Hand in hand with Katherine, Vince could go out to all the night spots- the casino and places in the city where the lights were bright. Perhaps a posh place dressed in neon lights that sold chocolate ice cream for he- "Mr. *Whitney*," and his new girlfriend. All those angry black guys from the basketball court with the cattle brands on their arms could wait on the two of them hand and foot after cleaning themselves up. Vince and Katherine could buy just one scoop of chocolate ice cream with two spoons, sit in the window of the restaurant and transfer a spoon of it from one of their mouths to the other's with a kiss. Along with all those angry black guys from the basketball court would be high school students from the plains to the city who were involved in every club known to man- those students in love with the sound of their own names, the football team, other students who had so little of a life outside of school that weekends meant two days of depression and mourning, the football coaches and most of all, Vince's father. *"Hey Dad, chip off th' old block, huh? Yeah, riiiiiiight!"*

As Vince and Katherine would sit in the window, under a plastic tree, k-i-s-s-i-n-g, everybody, at Vince's request, would turn their backs and look the other way. No peeking! As tempted as Vince felt to tell someone about his relationship with Katherine- anyone- he never told a soul.

Vince could never have understood or even comprehended the thought then of how Katherine needed someone or something to divert her attention from the fact she and Charles Whitney were not in love anymore. She never talked about anything like that to Vince, but she thought it might not be out of the ordinary to think he did not imagine something might be happening with her. He was after all, a smart guy. Heck, her husband was probably seeing someone else too, for all she knew. Even with all the time she and Vince shared, Katherine was already mentally preparing herself for the moment her husband would come through the door. No twitches of the eyes, no gulping in her throat, no crossing of her arms in defiance. There was no way Katherine would be so silly to think her husband would think things were normal upon his return if Vince were still around- that is, upon seeing him. She knew her relationship with Vince would have to be long over by then. Katherine had two months before her husband was due back from a cross-country trip giving lectures at major universities, he being a curator at one of the big museums in Washington D.C. As far as Vince knew, they were separated and never saw much of each other anymore. Katherine showed Vince some of the things he had written that sat in print on the shelves in their cottage and he held them in awe. *"By Charles Whitney, Assistant Curator."* Vince thought he must have been a very smart man to write books that were full of facts and so boring.

Vince had heard tell of it, but no one could prepare him for the nightmare which was the school prom. He was asked out four times by bookworm girls who, unknown to him, felt like his fall from grace might make him somewhat approachable. In truth, though he was handsome, Vince really had no idea of how other girls in the school actually noticed him. One girl who asked him to the prom was Shirley. Shirley weighed about two-hundred and seventy six and three quarter pounds and an odd number of grams at age seventeen and she was absolutely determined to get Vince as her date to the prom. She got off to a cracking start by never mentioning the football team and to Vince's own surprise, under the subtle pressure of her relentless determination, he almost said yes. Shirley was at the door to greet Vince at the end of every class he had, and she even showed up at his doorstep at home one Saturday afternoon after finding out where he lived, just like they were boyfriend and girlfriend. She showed up with three pieces of fried chicken- *where did she get that?!* the aroma of which was meant to entice him, along with a grape soda.

"Have you thought about my proposal?" she asked, smacking on a fried chicken leg.

"I've decided I'm not going to the prom this year," Vince replied, watching her wipe her greasy hands on her shirt.

"Aw come on Vince! I'll give you the rest of this chicken if you say yes!" Yeah, you heard her right. *I'm not hungry, but who said you had to be hungry to wanna eat?* Fortunately for Vince, he was not hungry.

Vince knew full well of how Katherine would never approve of him going out with another girl- one she had to look at on any given day through the halls of school, though she might have approved of Shirley, knowing he had no interest whatsoever in her and it would just be a platonic outing. Another girl who was just as determined as Shirley was Antionette, like the lady in the history books who got her head chopped off. Antionette was a light skinned black girl with freckles and red hair. She was slender, and she had great legs. What's more, she knew she had great legs. Vince found out Antionette was a friend of Shirley's, and it seemed he had come between them in some morbid, when it rains it pours kind of way.

"Now Vince, tell me the truth," Antionette said, standing in the hallway and tugging on his shirt. "You don't wanna take a fat girl like Shirley to the prom, and you know it."

"Go on," Vince said, as she rubbed herself up against him. She wore no stockings that day, and her vanilla wafer skin gave Vince ideas. Without thinking of consequences, Vince put his hands around her slender waist.

"Why don't you just come on and go with me," she said, putting both her arms around his neck. Katherine walked by, unknown to Vince, and saw them both. Anyone who saw them definitely got the impression Vince had a new girlfriend.

"I don't know if I want to go to the prom," Vince said, unsure.

She slowly kissed Vince on the cheek. *"Please?"*

It was a change of class, and Vince's locker happened to be at the other end of the school, away from Katherine's room. He noticed an empty classroom at the end of the hall, took Antionette into it, and closed the door. He knew kissing and holding her was wrong of him, but he wanted to see what it felt like to kiss a girl his own age again.

After about ten minutes, Vince finally realized he was late for Mrs. Gabby's class. Once he walked through the door and sat down, he saw Olivia on the other side of the room and she looked so small to him. So small.

"You're late Mr. Hill!" Mrs. Gabby called.

"Yes, ma'am, sorry!" Vince replied.

"One more time and you won't be allowed in!"

During the entire class, Olivia never lifted her head up. She did not pay any mind to Mrs. Gabby when she lectured, nor did she really move when they were told to open their books for the day's lesson. Her hair covered her face as if she was hiding behind it.

"Hi, are you all right?"

Olivia lifted her head, barely at the sound of Vince's voice. It was obvious to Vince her brown eyes had shed tears. One of her eyes were puffed and bruised.

"Olivia. What happened? Why are you crying?"

"We're not of the same yoke, you and I."

"That's why you're crying?" Vince asked in disbelief.

"I love you, that's all."

TWENTY-SIX

THE FOLLOWING SUNDAY MORNING in front of the sparse congregation, the drummer girl walked to the pulpit to pray:

"Dear Heavenly Father, I pray now,…for everyone here in this church. I pray for everyone here on this reservation. Forgive me Father, I'm not that good talking in front of people, but,….I pray that no one is ever hurt again here, or in the city, or in the world. I pray that the children here will always remain safe. I pray for my mother, I pray for the Pastor. I pray for everyone at school. I pray for my boyfriend heavenly father. Let him come back to me."

With a few snickers from the crowd in front of her, Olivia sat back down at her drum set.

The following Friday was the day of the prom and on that day Vince's separate lives- home, school and Katherine- became more distinct than ever. Katherine was assigned to be one of the mistresses of ceremonies. The affair was held in the school gymnasium because the school could not afford to have it anywhere else. Katherine knew Vince had received offers to go to the prom, but he wondered how she might react if she knew about Antionette.

"You know, you could have went to the prom if you wanted to, I would not have minded," Katherine offered from under running water inside her shower.

"I did not want to go!" Vince replied over the sound of the water.

"I mean really, you could have," Katherine said, stepping out of the shower and using a towel to dry her hair.

"Really, I-"

"Then why were you kissing that girl in the hallway?" she asked. "Does she mean anything to you?"

"What girl?" Vince asked, surprised.

"You don't have to lie to me!" Katherine shot back. "You know what girl!"

"That was nothing," Vince said. "She was just a friend!"

"You looked like more than friends to me! Tell me, did you sleep with her yet?!"

"No!"

"DID YOU SLEEP WITH HER?"

"No, I- I love *you!*....I'm sorry, it won't happen again!"

"I'm putting my butt on the line for you young man, don't forget it!"

"I won't, really!"

Katherine began letting Vince know of her duties at the function. Over and over again, she revealed how she might feel "funny," and even jealous, seeing him there, dancing with someone else- someone his own age. *There is no way I can enjoy being there, being a chaperone, seeing you there in the arms of someone else.* And so, there it was. Katherine said she loved Vince, which made things a bit easier for him when dealing with Antionette; why go out on a date and "play adolescent games" when he already had something stable?

For her own emotional insurance, Katherine asked Vince to stay at her house while she tended to her "chore" that was the prom. Vince sat in Katherine's bedroom beside her at her mirror, quiet, docile, watching her transform herself from a state of pure nakedness to a perfectly coifed, lovely woman sprinkled with shiny, multi-colored dust in a red and white patterned dress with iridescent white stockings and matching red heels. Katherine was a beautiful woman, and Vince did interrupt her transformation for a moment. She knew full well of the constant urge inside Vince to want to keep her in the bare state in which they began the afternoon.

After the door to the front of the cottage swung shut, Vince watched Katherine drive off through her living room window. Once he was alone, he sat still, while the tingling of the hanging wind chimes outside the door came to a gradual stop to complete silence. *We're not of the same yoke.* The wood floor inside the cottage still shimmered like water, even after all the times he had been there, while the heavy, still air within the cottage remained new to him. Ah, those naïve days, when Vince was unsure about Katherine's real intentions, seemed so far away. He walked into her classroom only looking for a place to hide from everyone, and got much more than he bargained for. As Vince looked around the house for the umpteenth time, every room bearing artifacts and antiques, he wondered where he fit into it all. *This is a local specimen, from the reservation. Soon, he'll be extinct.* One of her cats, which was sitting a short distance away and still unfamiliar with Vince, was even of a rare breed. Vince remembered Katherine saying the cat's previous owner was abusive, and how the animal did not trust easily. The cat stared, and Vince stared back, until its unfamiliarity with him became discomfort with all in the quiet surroundings. The feline would not budge, and somehow, it channeled to Vince how perhaps he was making a mistake. Vince stomped his foot on the floor toward the feline, and it arched its' back and hissed. He stood up from his chair and dove on the floor after it. It eluded him and ran into the bedroom to hide under the bed, which suited Vince fine. *I love you, that's all.* Just so he did not have to endure those eyes. Of all the things this woman seemed to have, why did Katherine want him? He had been nowhere, done nothing, and goodness, had not even taken his finals. All Vince understood was she loved him and he loved her. What did he really know about love?

Fast forwarding shadows grew longer within the cottage as Vince sat absorbing how different the small, quiet dwelling was from his own home. Vince stared at the shining wood floor, and could think of no part of the floor in his home that was not dirty. To his recollection, his father had worked hard over the years to make his house comfortable for them both, but he could never afford a floor like the one at his feet. Vince closed his eyes for a moment. *One of Olivia's eyes was puffed and bruised.* He saw his father in his mind, watching television and sneaking sips of cheap wine, which was all he did anymore when he was not at work in the city. Katherine's windows were clean and clear, letting in the last of the sun's rays, adorned with soft, sheer cotton curtains colored gold and crimson. They were beautiful against the polished oak surrounding almost everything in the house. He saw the covered, dingy windows in his home he wished Katherine to never see out of his embarrassment, blocking any light from the sun. *My dad's face had scratches all over it- but from what?* Vince opened his eyes to see the gigantic oak table he and Katherine had already shared quite a few dinners upon. He saw the bargain, dime store table in the middle of the eating area in his home, with its torn plastic top. One side of it he always had to hold down with his arm just to put down his plate of usually beans, rice, and perhaps bread. Sometimes slightly stale bread. Any kind of meat marked a special occasion. *There was a shoe- a girl's shoe- by the tires in the yard.* The grandfather clock standing in the corner was old, but very valuable and according to Katherine, symmetrically perfect. Handmade quilts laid in one corner, little cat toys sat in the middle of the floor, funny curved legs decorated the old chairs and books peppering the shelves with her husband's name on them made Vince wonder if Katherine really loved him. Then again, he had been away for quite a while. *How could they still be together?* He never thought for a moment of how Katherine could have been in some sort of pain. *There was a shoe- in the yard- I had seen that shoe before… Olivia's shoe.* "OLIVIA!"

Tears flowed from Vince's eyes as the day finally turned to night. As red orange hues outside slowly gave way to a shrouding ultramarine, the very thought of the unthinkable impaled his already confused heart, bloodying his mind. All of a sudden, sitting in the comfortable living room decorated with trinkets from all over the world, that place where above average white wine chilled in the refrigerator, that place where achievements of education and insight adorned the shelves, the feelings he thought he had for Katherine no longer mattered. He had to know the answer to the question which suddenly haunted him like thousands of ants and maggots crawling over his body, biting him, tasting him, in and out of every orifice and finally eating his brain and leaving behind no flesh. He grabbed his shoes and ran to the door, almost falling down on top of one of the cats that had grown comfortable with him, trying to put them on standing up. As he ran down the gravel driveway of the cottage, a car came up the hill. Vince ducked down into bushes by the road. It was Katherine's car. She drove by, parked in her garage, got out of the car and went into the house. Vince saw her in the window as she went from one room to another and as she did that, he began running. He ran as hard and as fast as he could, not even knowing which direction he was going in. He ran by the college campus, and saw the basketball court which before was filled with angry young black men. It was empty, under lights. With each and every step Vince took, his anger grew.

TWENTY-SEVEN

THE SPECTER STOOD in the middle of the reservation, sensing a depression hovering over its people. He listened to their pain and confusion, sensing the time had come to increase his minions toward deeds of darkness. The Specter would offer the people, through a series of their own transgressions, illusions of deliverance to a place where they would never feel alone again. Deliverance from the scorching, revealing light of the sun and from their own lies, anger, guilt, remorse, regret, embarrassment and hatred. Standing silent, his covered face surveyed all the possible avenues of sin the inhabitants of the plains took that night. The Specter brazenly stood in the middle of the main thoroughfare, unseen to all except those who sought him, those who became slowly dissatisfied with their lives over time. Those were the very souls on Sundays and any other day ending with the letter y who swore to give it the old college try, in public, but privately grew tired of waiting for The Lord to scoop them out of the midst of their own problems, without offering him any assistance. Those were the people who became open to the growing ennui inside them; a state of mind equivalent to being lukewarm toward the very idea of gaining self-esteem. A perspective as deadly as becoming accustomed to everyday death and dying by violence, thinking it normal. They were people who trudged each day to and fro from jobs sucking on their dignity- situations where they had to prove themselves to strangers everyday for the monetary equivalent of change between the cushions of a prosperous community, with that amount of money never quite being enough to build dreams of their own. Perhaps they could live within a fantasy, seeing themselves off on a beach somewhere, or perhaps even living in the city- anywhere but the reservation where the people there reminded them all too much of themselves. *Hey! What's wrong with that? Everything under the sun, that's what!*

Mr. Trotter had not been home in three days, thinking not once of his wife who wondered and worried over where he was. Part of the time he spent in the casino, part of another time he spent with some woman whose name he could not even recall. *Hey man, who really knows anyone?* No matter where he was, within all the time he tried to spend where his paycheck would take him, there was The Specter, whispering in his ear: *Why do you need anyone at all? With me, you never have to go home. With me, you can be free of having to answer to anyone. You can free yourself of this crude shell called a body and experience true pleasure. You do not ever have to get up and go to work, or to live up to a word you wish you had not given, or to even wash away an offensive stench for those around you who work to hide their own stenches. Why do you persist, playing this game? COME WITH ME!!*

Inside the casino, Mr. Trotter looked into his empty glass he wanted filled with another shot of liquor. He had not one more red cent. He had gotten paid three days before and decided to just let out all the things he was feeling with barely an ounce of sleep. He no longer saw the point of going home, to the same woman who did not know or appreciate the finer things in life which meant drinking and occasional drugs. There were plenty of prostitutes in the city who spoke and even taught that language however, and for the previous two days for him, class was in session. He could, in his mind, be a renegade and still live up to his responsibilities, other people did it, he was sure of it. *Yeah, other people do it, why can't I?* Where he expected freedom in dark corners, he only found guilt. One last binge before he gave it up for good. He saw his wife's face in the glass, yeah. It was no guarantee she was even going to take him back. *Got money for a drink?* He would get on his knees, make it really special this time. She would not be able to say no.

Walking out into the early night air from the casino, he barely remembered his way home. Suddenly, nothing mattered anymore when he fell face down on the side of the road, never to see his wife again. *You call this deliverance? All I see is blackness.*

Olivia sat in her modest little room with her mother right outside on a chair watching television, silent and wondering where was her god and how could he have forsaken her. She still saw Vince's father drunken, lecherous face, evil and stinking in her nightmares. *Mama, I got hit by mistake- ha, can you believe it, a ball someone threw while I was in gym class. Can you believe that?* Unknown to Olivia, The Specter stood off to the side of her bed as she lay, waiting for an opportunity to whisper in her ear. Nothing would please him more than to have one of The Lord's faithful turn away from him in sorrow, in hopelessness, in pain. The kind of pain allowing him to sway her for all time. Perhaps into the streets with her, hand in hand with another transgression she would surely find comfort in; anger and the inability to forgive. *"Come with me..come with me..you never have to suffer the pain of this life ever again."*

Olivia rose and sat on her bed. Looking out toward her window at the night sky, there were no more tears. "I will never go the way of darkness, away from you. I invite you in now, touch my heart, stay with me. I will forever believe in you." The Specter turned his back on her and disappeared.

What of the abusive coach who made the boys in football practice fall to their knees in pain and cry out to the heavens, because the world never did what he thought it should do? He justified his actions only with wins and losses, pushing aside the lives ruined by his wrath. What of him, the man who justified his own existence by seeing others in pain? *"I will be by your side, to lie for you when you need me."*

What of the students at Redemption, the ones who did not even know they didn't know they hated each other simply for being black and poor? *"I will keep you in a perpetual state of self hatred, of lust, of defiance and of darkness. For you, the skies will forever remain dark, blocking out the light of the moon and the sun. Those who weep for you will never find a way to reach you; none will be able to enter and none of you will be able to leave."*

What of the drunken father, who committed an act so heinous, damaging a young girl's perspective, her trust, her mind, her memory, her spirit- with no amount of conscience? The one who hoped to live vicariously through his son- one with whom he will never share a language of love? *"Behind me you will stay, shrouded in darkness. I will go forth and speak for you, lie for you and protect you."*

What of the young man who runs toward his destiny- to confront his father- the one who finally came to realize his existence, his purpose within the risings and settings of the sun? The young man who armed himself with a dangerous truth that belies his years- the one who broke away from believing what he sees as real? The one who never believed in The Evil? *"I will go to him, to sway his mind- to change the truth he thinks he knows. In a time and place of darkness where he will never be able to see his own face, his will shall succumb before mine, and my victory shall be complete."*

What about the Pastor who even though he was unsure of himself from the onset, remains strong and ready to lead his people out of the spiritual bondage and self hatred they have grown accustomed to? How can such a man be made to believe in the staleness of apathy, the lukewarm taste of indifference and spreading the absolute zero temperature of a lack of compassion? *"His spirit remains strong. I will destroy all around him, that he may lose hope."*

What of those in the city who worship no god, but gold, silver and all things tangible? Those who have become accustomed to seeing their own likenesses in the mirror- likenesses they have painted and held up in such vanity to the point where they now believe in themselves and only themselves? *"They remain on a course with me. Though their clothes be slowly shredded by the pestilence of greed, their nakedness will become acceptable to one another. I will hide from them the rust their riches have collected, so they will not bear witness against the thing I have built."*

As the Specter continued surveying the land from the plains to the city, he felt Vince's urgency and anger from where he stood.

With every step Vince took, he felt the pain of turning his back on Olivia when she needed him. *How could I be so blind?* His fists clenched at the thought of his father taking advantage of Olivia. *I'm gonna kill you.* Olivia was his girlfriend, not Mrs. Whitney. Sweat ran from Vince's forehead, each desperate bead tingling upon his skin. He ran through a grove of trees, away from the main highway. As he ran, Vince looked up to the skies. The light of the moon did not reach the ground through the trees until he saw an opening leading to a clearing. He remembered then some of the sights Mrs. Whitney passed in her car each and every time he ventured into the city with her.

Vince reached a barren field at the edge of the trees, a dead, abandoned part of the city. He stopped for just a moment to catch his breath in the humid night. He knew he would have to risk going through parts of the city where he might be exposed and even stopped by police. "Perhaps the night can cover me, shield me," he thought.

At that moment, something or someone was behind him. He turned, but there was no one- the field was bare, lined by trees and within the trees, not a sound. Vince stood still, even stopping his breathing for moments to listen. He looked through the yellowed field and at the trees all around him away from the city lights. *Something is here- someone is watching me.* Vince turned to run again toward the highway, and he was taken aback by the hooded, ghastly figure standing before him, exposing himself a second time- there in the field and with his father before in the car through the pouring rain.

The thing was almost seven feet tall and barely visible under the light of the moon. The vision Vince saw of the thing appeared and re-appeared as if by way of a transmission. In and out, it blurred several times and then finally became clear. Vince could not see a face within its dark shroud, but there was an aroma at first, like red clay. Then the aroma turned to the odor of dirt- then of bodies decaying, of things dead or dying. At the feet of the thing, many, many maggots crawled upon its garment. Vince could almost hear them, gnawing at what was left of flesh. This beast, this thing in front of him, held out the remains of its human hand in friendship. It too, was covered with maggots.

"Your journey is over now- come with me and you will feel no more guilt," The Specter whispered.

"I-I saw you," Vince blurted out, shivering from a sudden chill in the thick air. "You- you were in my father's car- that night it rained- I saw you through the window! Who are you?!"

"I am no one," The Specter replied. *"I am everyone. I am responsible for the location of your people. I am the reason they are backed into a corner and wallow in sin. I am fear, doubt and the lack of courage summoning you now. I am sickness, I am death, I am the very reason you feel pain."*

"This is some kind of trick- some kind of special effects city trick somebody is playing on me!" Vince yelled. "It has to be a trick! You're not real!"

At that moment, a crushing blow came upon Vince, knocking him down, pinning him to the ground, smashing his face into the dirt. Upon the ground he saw how maggots from The Thing had already begun to quickly make their way toward him. Something then grabbed him and pulled him up to his feet. When Vince looked down, he saw his feet were not touching the ground. Tears streamed from his face, first from fear, then from pain, then from anger.

"Come with me young one and stand at my side. Do my bidding and I shall reward you with riches you will not be able to count," The Thing uttered.

"You brought the flood- you killed all those people- you took advantage of my girlfriend- why?"

"I will tell you what you have envisioned with your friend- the girl- is true. I know you go now to confront your father."

"Yeah, you're right," Vince blurted, still floating. "What do you want with me? You are powerful enough to do all these crazy things- you can do what you want!"

"I need a trumpeter; someone young and full of life like you in this world to sing my praises. I need you to convince many others that I am real."

"No! I know enough to know you are a liar! If you can do all this, what is stopping you from keeping your word?"

"I will offer you a test."

"A test? Come on, man! I get enough of that at school!"

"I can turn back the hands of time. I can give you your friend back, make her whole again, erase the deeds of your father."

"You mean like it never happened at all?"

"You will encounter the test before you reach the door of your father. If you survive this test, I will restore your friend to the way she was, before your father took advantage. If you fail, then you will stand at my side to do

my bidding. The reservation will go on and your people will wallow on in transgressions every day until there are no more of them left."

"What about my father?"

Vince fell to the ground, his face in the dirt. He looked up and the thing, the evil, was gone. *This is a dream, it has to be- none of this is real.* Vince looked down at his feet and saw maggots still crawling, looking for something to feed on.

David sat asleep and sweating in front of the television in his filthy chair at home, covered in the odor of a blanket that had not been washed in months. In his dream, he knew full well Vince was coming, because The Specter told him so. The Specter promised to stand by him, his loyal but ignorant subject whom he had promised riches beyond belief to. Within the texture of David's dreams who knew- he could play the position of running back on the football team of all time, amassing more yardage than anyone who ever played. According to David, one thing was for certain, as a single maggot crawled up the blanket covering him, he would "never need nobody else" cause he had the one friend who would stand by him, take care of him and love him when no one else would.

TWENTY-EIGHT

VINCE BROKE INTO a slow trot, still in a state of disbelief, but believing everything he had seen and heard from The Thing who stood in front of him. *A test?* Lights from what appeared to be a commercial part of the city drew closer to the field with every step he took. Vince climbed over a fence separating the field from the highway and ran across the road. There, he stood on clean, manicured streets under gleaming street lights and tall buildings. He walked in a direction he thought might take him to the city limits. "Perhaps I can get a ride with someone going back to the reservation," he thought.

Walking within buildings around him almost stretching to the sky, he heard what sounded like a crowd. He drew closer to the sound and a great light in the short distance became even brighter as the sound drew near. Vince turned a corner to what looked like an opening, a square, in the middle of the metropolis. A huge crowd of mostly whites stood all around, being entertained by something. Vince noticed he was not the only black in the crowd; there were businessmen, men who wore ties and suits- black people he had never seen on the reservation laughing and cheering within the majority of the throng. As Vince drew closer to the noise no one around really noticed him at first. He began smelling an odor in the air like something old and stale. He made his way through the crowd to see what had everyone so entertained.

The young black men he had played with earlier on the basketball court- the ones who threatened him with angry faces, all danced around in the middle of the crowd with colorful beenies atop each of their heads. They danced with their arms out by their sides with their chins jutted out- like apes. "Whoop-whoop! Whoop-whoop!" was the sound they all made in unison. They all brandished plastic, permanent smiles. Though they carried out the motions with much vigor, the looks in each of their eyes was a sad one, indicative of a fatigue resulting from captivity. The whites and few blacks in the crowd laughed and laughed all around the dance while Vince stood gazing on the verge of tears- momentarily forgetting his destination. He saw the looks in their eyes- one that said they just wanted to stop. *Please, can you make it stop?* Vince outstretched his hand toward them- those who only hours before meant him harm- and their pain was tangible.

"GET HIM!" one within the crowd said, pointing and looking directly at Vince. Vince turned and ran in any direction. He looked back to see who was behind him and every one of the young black men were hot on his heels, still wearing their beenies, still smiling.

"GET HIM! GET HIM!" The crowd yelled at Vince from behind. *Is this the test?*

Vince ran around parked cars, around buses and through sidewalk cafes with the young black men not far behind. Moments later, he came upon another crowded street where many white couples all walked hand in hand toward one direction, at first appearing to be out for romantic evenings. Vince ducked and weaved through them all and into a corner store. The store was small and he went through it to a back aisle and ducked as the young black men ran by outside. An Oriental woman came out from behind a counter enclosed by a thick pane of glass. In her hand was a gun.

"GET OUT MY STORE!" she yelled.

"Ma'am, these people were chasing-"

"I DON'T CARE!" she yelled, waving the gun toward the door. "YOU BLACK! YOU BAD PERSON! YOU DON'T BUY NOTHING!"

Vince stood up from ducking. He stood, only looking at the woman, wondering how she could be so mean. He was shocked at the fear she showed of him in her eyes. As the woman shivered, Vince noticed the gun was a toy.

"You go now, please," she said, with her voice lowering. She was defenseless. Without a word, Vince walked out the door.

To the left and right, the young black men were nowhere in sight as couples continued walking and holding hands, oblivious to Vince's plight. Vince trotted along the side of them, at first to hide, then he began wondering where they all were going. Around one corner they all went, ending up at a church brightly lit under the night sky. When they all got to the door of the building, they stopped and stood in line. A banner hung over the church door that read "Reveal your most inner selves to your God." Vince began running, away from them, chasing time and looking for a way out of the city and away from the people there. Away from the mayhem, he remembered his anger, his purpose; to make his father pay for what he did. He broke away into another part of the city adorned in neon lights of all colors with women wearing painted faces and short skirts. Some walked around, some stood here and there under street lamps. Vince passed by and underneath blinking, colorful, fluorescent lights against the sound of coins falling everywhere. Amid the many patrons who passed by and around him, he saw only few faces through hats and even shades. The many electronic hues emitting from the giant strobe rendered Vince colorless; he was the same as everyone else and no one cared about anything he had been running from. No one asked any questions and no one even noticed him as they were too concerned about winning and losing money, too concerned about hiding identities, concealing faces. Vince began feeling safe within the transgressors, like no one was watching him. A woman dressed in a revealing outfit made of patent leather stopped him by putting her hand against his chest. At first, her painted face and the light colored long hair falling over her face as she moved was beautiful, seductive. Through the strobe, Vince saw her eyes were a cerulean blue of a clear daytime sky without a cloud. Her hair descended upon her shoulders like golden wheat, her skin fine like milk. She began speaking to Vince, without even opening her mouth. *"Come with me,"* she said. *"Come with me, and you'll never have to feel guilt again. You will never have to endure another test as long as you live."*

"Test?" Vince thought.

At that moment, her porcelain face quickly turned to maggots, her blue eyes to jet black marbles. Vince fell back, brushing maggots off his chest from her touch. He ran away, faster, faster, even though his legs were weary, he kept running. He came upon a main road, a road leading to the gate of the city where guards stood. As Vince waited alongside a wall wondering how to get out, a large truck came by carrying black workers out of the city back to the reservation. Its cargo had an open back where Vince saw the workers sitting inside. As the truck stopped in a line of vehicles inching toward the gate, Vince jumped into the back. Inside, the men were tired from the menial, physical labor they had been performing all day. Many of them had eyes half shut and covered with dirt, some were asleep. There were others in the front of the truck's bed talking to each other about just wanting to get back to the reservation with their weekend checks before the casino and the liquor stores closed. Vince sat on the floor of the truck within them all. The truck cleared the gate, and for what seemed like a few short moments, Vince fell asleep.

Pastor Carson stood within the empty folding chairs of his church and looked around at the bare cinder block walls. He felt there was something odd about that quiet night. He had seen it on the empty roads as the only sound in the night was the casino's bells and whistles off in the distance. He went back outside and gazed into the night's thick, humid air. Clouds had formed overhead and Carson could smell the rain coming. He turned back around toward the modest building that was the church which still did not look much different from when Pastor Jenkins preached his last sermon. Sure, there were finally some robes for the choir made from old clothes instead of brown paper bags. The numbers of the congregation increased here and there, but he knew in his heart how they still only sought to be entertained. Go on too long on Sundays, and he was a crashing boar. If the sermon was too short, they would say he wasn't prepared. As he stood silent, he realized how he had become nothing more than an entertainer. *You're preaching to the choir, man! By the way, thank you, I'll be here all week.* He was nothing more than a clown, spewing fancy rhetoric within a sea of futile apathy, with those on the plains all laughing and laughing at their own demise. *Come see the guy who took Pastor Jenkins' place. He's okay. He'll give a word here and there, something to hear before we eat scraps.*

As Frank Carson stood alone, silent and finally accepting his role as Pastor, he began thinking he had perhaps made a mistake going onto the city channel. His intention in the beginning was to reach as many as possible, only to end up appearing late on weekend nights in between hobgoblins and derelicts who spit profanity into microphones over beats the masses longed to hear. The people on the reservation so desperately wanted to follow someone, anyone, but all they ever followed in the end were cretinous cuss words. *Are there any other kind?* Carson was one inside the screen in a long line of vendors, freaks, and eighty-nine cent special effects. Days however, turned into weeks with Pastor Carson only fatigued at the thought of driving the long road yet again. As he stood outside the building that was his church, he realized how he had lost touch with the reservation itself as he chased celebrity status. The weight of the world sat squarely on his shoulders. If there was a child to mentor, it was up to him or else it would never happen. He had to be the one to turn the other cheek, to not feed into the hopelessness of a perspective of low self-esteem being passed around the reservation like candy of good quality. The people on the plains were set for self-destruct. He knew full well how the numbers who believed in The Lord had to increase, as he felt The Specter making his move to claim lost souls. Overhead, there was a low rumble of thunder and with it, a light rain began to fall. Pastor Carson knew that night, the people were in a battle for their lives, and something had to be done. Just then, at his side, he looked down and saw Ronnie, looking up to him and smiling, wiping raindrops away from his face. The boy extended his hand, and his father took it. *Fight him, daddy. You're strong and I know you can win.*

"I'll win son, for you, me and the good people of these plains."

The role of Pastor was his, but so was the never ending fight with The Specter.

TWENTY-NINE

WHAT BEGAN AS a light rain, soon turned into a downpour and everything under the clouds, even the dirt roads, glistened under the night sky. As the truck carrying the workers rolled up to the gate, Vince was still asleep. Once inside the gate, he was awakened by the workers exiting the back of the truck, slipping, falling, splashing and running for the lights of the casino.

Vince stood alone on one side of a road past the gate, under the many raindrops hitting his face and amid the sound of them pelting the surface of the dry, thirsty land at his feet. Across the road from him sat a bunch of belongings- broken furniture, boxes and a heap of clothes. Everything began sinking into the puddle of water forming underneath it. People he had never even seen before- a man, a woman and two children- were huddled together under the deluge; they had been evicted. Vince wondered should he ask if they needed help or not, but how could he help them? The children cried to each other within the storm, but Vince had bigger concerns on his mind, namely revenge. *Is this family before me a test?* He turned away from them. With that, Vince began running.

That night, many people on the reservation gambled and drank the night away with no thoughts of what may come. Losing money they did not have was an idea which never occurred to them, rather, it was the chase- the thought of winning spurring them on to nothingness. The Specter watched it all and was delighted. He was more happy though, with everyone on the plains hating one another and never coming together on anything for as long as they would live. One worker fresh from the city truck laughed as coins fell out of a slot machine into his dingy hat. The cash had the appearance of an avalanche of good luck and his eyes widened at the sight of the gleaming silver. There were a few choleric ones who had sank deeper into the abyss of losing who swore to wait outside for the man to leave with his winnings. *Knock him over the head, take his money, then come back and maybe I'll win. I'll play the same machine- perhaps it will bring me luck like it did him.* Drinks flowed, with tomorrow a thing to be considered only with the rising of the sun.

The odor of smoke began filling the casino and slowly, one looked at another, who looked at another. Fire. People began walking around, looking to see if the place was indeed on fire. Most of the people on the reservation, from Coach Turk to laborers who had come in on the late truck from the city stopped gambling for a moment at a sound. It was a loud sound, like gunshots. Some of them walked outside into the pouring rain to see Pastor Carson, standing atop a large box in the middle of the lot where only few cars were parked. He was busy setting off fireworks over a fire he had made from the casino's huge garbage can. At the foot of the large box, children of the gamblers inside stood all around, holding sparklers that glistened in the rain.

"Have you lost your mind?!" one man yelled. "What are you doing? These are all our kids! Who gave you permission to take our kids out in this mess?!" Everyone in the casino was either outside, in the doorway of the casino, or looking out its bathroom windows. Perfect. Seeing how he had his audience, Pastor Carson lit many more sparklers around the box.

"You gave me permission," Pastor countered, when you chose to leave them at home to raise themselves! They miss you- they miss you all!"

"You're crazy!" another shouted.

"Will there be any tonight?!" Pastor continued, over cries of anger. "Will there be any tonight who will give their lives to Jesus Christ- if so, please step forward!"

"Go to hell!" one shouted.

"YOU PEOPLE HERE HAVE ALREADY ACCOMPLISHED THAT! THANK YOU!" Carson screamed back. "You have accomplished that for you, for me and for your children's future! You can invest in this place, but you cannot invest in your own seed, your young! Look at them- how long are you all going to continue ignoring them?! They need you- not a pile of coins- and not mommy and daddy coming in so drunk you forget to tuck them in at night, or forgetting to say 'I love you.' This has been going on here now, for years, to the point where they think it all is normal. What do you all expect to find in this place of lies? Love? Understanding? A future? God? Tell me, does The Lord come to you in coins or dollar bills? Do you see him in your drinks at the bar as you try to forget how you slave your days away to people who do not even appreciate your worth? Stop looking for approval in the wrong places! It's inside you already, and in the faces of your children! Has anyone told any of you how you yourselves are worthy to be loved today? Anyone?! If not, let me say now- I love you! I love you! I LOVE YOU!"

"Why don't you go on home, you crazy fool!" Coach Turk spat from within the crowd that began laughing in ridicule of Pastor Carson.

"GO HOME!" several in the crowd shouted behind Coach Turk, who led them in laughter.

All that comes out of your mouth is Bible stuff- the history of Jewish people!" Coach Turk laughed. "They have nothing to do with us- here! This is a different place, a different time! Do you even know your own history?!"

"HE'S NO FOOL!" Olivia Henry shouted back with her long hair plastered over her wet, shining face, standing beside her mother a short distance across the road. They lived nearby and both of them had come out of the house and into the rain to see what all the commotion was about. "He's my Pastor! You- you can stand there, and try your best to ruin young men's lives- like Vince's- young men who had the courage to stand up to you. You're a coward, just like the rest of the grown folks here in this, place or whatever you wanna call it. You all are nothing but slaves to the city with no vision of your own! I don't want anything to do with the likes of you! I will fall to my knees and pray to my God that he spares us from his wrath for all the times you have only thought about yourselves and no one else!"

"NOW IS THE TIME!" Pastor Carson shouted. "Now is the time for us to come together! To love one another and care for one another!" The crowd fell silent within the falling water, while the bells of the casino rang on from inside. The fire he started had burned out and there was only smoke and wet ashes left behind.

"I stand now, in the face of the one who would spread evil through this place and through your hearts. You cannot see him, but I tell you, having done battle with him all my life, he is as real as you and I standing here, as the water falls upon us. We stand here now, husbands who have not been husbands, wives who feel only sorrow and loneliness day by day!" Mrs. Trotter stood within the crowd and shook her head in agreement.

"Our children govern themselves- at the doors of darkness! People, the water falling upon our heads now can be a signal- a new beginning! I'm sorry folks, yes he's right. I am a fool, and that is my history, which can be summed up in a couple of sentences. I am a fool who cares for you, and you and all of you. My history is, I am a naked, ignorant fool who God decided to give a second and third chance to. I thought, perhaps, we could make the most of it together- perhaps we can all find our own history, together. There it is, I'm only trying to make the most of it. Forgive me. I won't bother any of you again."

With that, Pastor Carson got down from the box, and walked away, through the crowd and off into the distance, through the pelting rain. Some people went home, some went back to the casino.

THIRTY

His father's house was in sight through the thick deluge, and Vince no longer felt tired. The front door was in his sight. *Kick it in? Test? What test? That thing, in the field, was all my imagination. No one has confronted me, there has been no test. Who? The chasers? I got past them! The people on the side of the road who got put out of their home? Did I pass it already? It must have been a dream!*

As his father's front yard became completely clear in front of Vince, he made the decision to break the door in quickly. His father had to pay for what he did, and he was going to make him do just that. Then, a blackening blow, from something, came from nowhere through the rain, sending Vince down into the mud. He cleared his head and looked up to see who or what had hit him.

Mike Chambers. As he stood in the rain over Vince breathing heavily with his muscular arms flexed, his eyes were ablaze with the color of anger and the power of fire. It was him, and then again, it wasn't.

"I told you," Mike groveled in a voice that was not his own, *"I was going to get you when the time was right! Guess what? The right time is tonight!"*

Through blurred vision from the deluge, Vince looked off to the side of Mike at a hooded figure only standing still.

Bigger, stronger, faster. I am weary from the chase, from so much running! My arms and legs are like rubber against this- an adversary with fire in his eyes! Oh God, how can I triumph?

Mike moved like lightning and took a swing at Vince, his massive arm cutting through the rain like a saw. Vince ducked, narrowly escaping the blow and grabbing Mike's legs, trying to knock him down. He stood like a post of iron. Vince's feet slipped in the mud. Vince quickly rolled away and stood up to face him. *Now what?*

"It's you in there, isn't it?" Vince called out. "You're that evil thing who wants everyone to be as miserable as him. All this can't be about what happened in football practice! I will never listen to you, or believe your lies, or be as miserable as you, no matter what you do!"

"ARRRRGH!!" Mike called out in a flash of rage and he was on Vince in a second, grabbing him by the throat, choking him. The grip of his hands felt like a vice. Vince began passing out, but just then he thought of Olivia and how she believed in God with all her heart. "God! Help me!" Vince called out. "Help me God!"

Just before Vince's vision faded to black, he felt Mike's grip loosen around his neck. He then watched Mike fall to the mud. When he looked up, it was the Pastor from the church.

"Young man, I heard your cry!" Pastor Carson said. I am aware of what you face. I am here to help you." With that, Vince passed out.

Vince awakened in his room, in his lumpy bed, so familiar. Through the dingy windows of his home, the morning sun's light shone. He arose from bed and walked out to the frayed dining table where his father had cereal and milk waiting for him. His father was clean, shaven and upright, looking into their old mirror on the wall one last time with a jacket in his hand, ready to leave for work.

"See you later son, I gotta go ta' work early today. I'll try ta' bring you something back from th' city! Have a good day, I love you!" He then left and closed the door behind him.

It was his house all right, and as old and worn as everything was they owned within it, Vince could not ever remember the house being so clean. He began readying himself for school.

Once Vince got to Redemption, he sat in Mrs. Gabby's geometry class with a vigor he had never felt before.

"Class!" Mrs. Gabby addressed, "Please welcome our new student- Olivia Henry. Olivia, where are you from?"

"New York, ma'am!" she replied.

Vince turned around to see a girl with fair skin and long, shining hair. She took the seat right in front of him. Vince stared at her in disbelief.

"Hello," she offered.

"Hi, Olivia," Vince replied with a certain familiarity, to which she appeared puzzled.

"Um, Olivia, I don't mean to startle you but I want to ask, would, would you like to have lunch with me today?"

"Uh, sure, sure I'll have lunch with you," Olivia responded.

The two of them met for lunch and talked about everything under the sun. Vince felt so relaxed with her. In the middle of the conversation, Vince noticed a small silver cross around Olivia's neck.

"Olivia, do you go to church?" Vince asked.

"Yes Vince, yes I do," she responded. "My mother raised me in the church. Why do you ask?"

"We have a church here, did you know that?"

"Yeah, I play drums for the church band."

"Wow, well I wanna ask you, could I come to church with you on Sunday?"

Olivia lit up. She had never had a boy ask her that question before. "Of course, I would love it!" she exclaimed.

"You know, Olivia, I like you so much already and, I know if I want to be with you at all, we have to be of the same yoke, right?"

"Y-Yes, we do Vince, I know."

"It just so happens that I want to get saved. I want it for me- really- but I like you too."

Olivia's eyes welled with tears as she looked directly into Vince's. *Is this boy sincere?*

That Sunday, Olivia came to pick Vince up in an old car bellowing smoke. As they rode to The Baptist Church of the Reservation, the aroma of flowers after the rain showers the night before filled the air. Vince sat in the back seat holding hands with Olivia and as they both looked out the window, the blossoming trees were so beautiful to Vince, like he had never seen them before.

The scene inside the church was energetic as Olivia took her seat at the drums and the band began to play. The crowd jumped in delight at the sound of music worshipping God. In the pulpit, a man wearing a long robe who appeared to be the Pastor of the church looked directly at Vince. *Maybe he knows I am new.* As the Pastor continued looking, he smiled and nodded his head. Just then, a familiarity came over Vince, as if he knew the man, as if he had even fought a battle with him of some kind. As The Pastor smiled, Vince immediately felt a certain bond, and he knew by choosing to get saved from sin, he was making the right choice. At that, The Pastor turned his attention toward a young boy, taking him in his arms and laughing as the music played, as the people jumped and worshipped. As the boy sat right beside The Pastor, it was obvious to Vince that the boy loved his daddy with all his heart.

The sun was almost down behind the grocery store, and Old Mister Sheppard still sat under his tree. I wanted to cry, because I thought Tynette had moved for sure. I wanted to ask God, if there was one, to please send her out to me. Please let that beautiful girl come out and play with me. The sun looked as if it was sitting right on top of the building and I began thinking I might not come back there after that day.

"FRANKIE!!" a voice from beside the apartment building yelled. A girl's voice.

"TYNETTE!!" I jumped from the swing and ran through the weeds to go hug her. When I got close, she started running around and laughing, making me chase her. Out of the corner of my eye, I saw Old Mister Sheppard nodding with his pipe and I also saw how the boys who liked to fight across the way in the field were no longer there. For once, there was peace and quiet. I caught Tynette and wrapped my arms around her from behind so she could not run away again. Within the silence, we both laughed and laughed.

Printed in the United States
222134BV00001B/1/P